"We haven't done the talking part yet," Sean said

"We will…" Laurel rose up on her toes, took his face in her hands and kissed him. No gentle peck, no teasing come-on. She flat out kissed him. A heartbeat later he was kissing her back.

Sean pushed his hips against hers. "Damn, I still don't even know you."

"I don't know you, either. So explain why this feels like one of the rightest things I've ever done." Laurel laughed a little. "God, I hope I don't feel like an idiot for saying that come morning."

Sean leaned in and kissed her, only gently this time. "I don't want any regrets," he murmured. Although he already knew he'd have a boatload. Not for making love to her. No, never. He was going to regret not having more time with her here on the island. Time to get past making love…and falling into it.

Dear Reader,

I was thrilled to hear that the *Men of Courage* anthology was so well received that our editors wanted each of us to write a spin-off story. Brett, my hero from "Buried!," has a great set of siblings that I was dying to write about. But none so much as his older brother, U.S. marshal Sean Gannon. Of course, given Sean's dedication to job and country, he'd probably have preferred me to leave him alone. All the more reason to complicate things for him!

So I put a damsel in distress directly in his path, one he wasn't going to be able to walk away from. The problem? Laurel Patrick is the type of woman who prefers to solve her own problems, thank you. Did I mention she was a district court judge? Sean suspects she's in more trouble than she can handle...and he's not backing off. Sparks fly, pulses pound, passion flares. All the ingredients I love best!

I hope you enjoy Sean and Laurel's story as much as I enjoyed writing it.

Happy reading,

Donna Kauffman

Books by Donna Kauffman

HARLEQUIN TEMPTATION
828—WALK ON THE WILD SIDE
846—HEAT OF THE NIGHT
874—CARRIED AWAY

HARLEQUIN BLAZE
18—HER SECRET THRILL
46—HIS PRIVATE PLEASURE
69—AGAINST THE ODDS

DONNA KAUFFMAN

SEAN

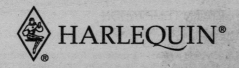

HARLEQUIN®

TORONTO • NEW YORK • LONDON
AMSTERDAM • PARIS • SYDNEY • HAMBURG
STOCKHOLM • ATHENS • TOKYO • MILAN • MADRID
PRAGUE • WARSAW • BUDAPEST • AUCKLAND

This book is for Mark, Mitch, Spence & Brandon
My own personal heroes.

ISBN 0-373-69134-3

SEAN

Copyright © 2003 by Donna Jean.

Visit us at www.eHarlequin.com

Printed in U.S.A.

1

"WHO'D HAVE THOUGHT I'd be the first one of the Gannon men to tie the knot, eh?" Brett Gannon slung an arm around his older brother's shoulders and tipped back the last of a beer.

Sean grinned and finished his beer in one long pull. "Well, Clay is too busy dating his way through the University of Louisiana's cheerleading squad. And I knew it wasn't going to be me."

"Yeah, you're already married. How is the Marshals Service treating you anyway?" he teased. "Still exciting as those early days, when the romance was fresh? Can we expect the pitter-patter of little agents' feet anytime soon?"

Sean just grinned. "Yep, just as soon as I get through with my next class out at Beauregard. I'm sure my recruits are all going to make me very proud." His grin widened. "Or die trying."

Brett winced. "Glad I don't have to impress you."

Sean looked across the yard at Haley, at how happy she was. "You already have," he said quite seriously. He grinned when Brett gave him a surprised look. "But I will admit I thought you'd play a much wider field first."

Brett shot him his trademark cheeky grin. "In the end, it's just more green grass."

Sean looked back to Haley, radiant in the simple

white gown she'd chosen. "You did find yourself a right sunny patch of it, that's for certain." He glanced back at the middle Gannon brother in time to see Brett staring at his wife of less than one hour, so totally besotted it should have made Sean want to roll his eyes and shake his head. Instead it created an odd little twinge somewhere down deep inside him.

Brett noticed his brother's frown. "Is it weird for you? Because you used to date her? I mean, it *was* several lifetimes ago."

"And I suppose that crush you had on her back then was just some youthful infatuation, huh?" Sean countered.

Brett was unabashed. "The only thing youthful was my inability to hold on to her. But I always knew a good thing when I saw it."

"Unlike me, I suppose." Sean had said it jokingly, but there was a thread of honesty in the statement that caused that twinge to sharpen.

"Hey, I figure you did us both a favor. She didn't want to marry the U.S. Marshals Service. And eventually I did grow up and learned to hang on to something good when I had it."

"Yeah," Sean said, his gaze shifting back to Haley, serene and calm amid the other members of the raucous Gannon clan. "And may I say, when you hang, you hang with the best." He looked back at his brother. "I'm happy for you, Brett. Truly. And I hope like hell you contribute more to the Gannon legacy than those four-legged animals you work with."

"What, you having a yearning to play uncle? Carly's brand-new little squaller isn't enough for you?"

"Carly's baby terrifies me," he said quite seriously.

"Yeah, I know," Brett said, admitting his terror for the first time. "How can something so tiny have such huge lungs?"

It wasn't the screaming that bothered him. Sean had been referring to those perfect little delicate fingers and those teeny, tiny toes. How was a guy supposed to hold something like that without breaking it? Yet his younger sister had taken to motherhood as if she'd been born to it. And, truthfully, out of the five Gannon kids, she was the one most suited for the job. Although watching the way Brett was making googly eyes at his bride, he thought it wouldn't be too long before he had another squalling niece or nephew. Brett had always been an animal lover, hence his job training rescue dogs. And Sean had to admit, the animals loved him. As far as he was concerned, that qualified him as well as anyone to be a parent.

"Ha," Brett was saying. "You just figure if Haley and I can distract Mom and Dad by popping out babies on some kind of routine schedule, they'll forget their two oldest offspring are still unwed." He snorted. "Good luck."

"Nah, we'll just sic 'em on Clay."

Brett leveled a look at him. "Are you kidding? He *is* a baby."

"True. Having him make more would just be redundant," Sean said, making them both laugh.

"So, you still thinking about taking the job at Camp Beauregard? Doing the full-time trainer thing for our country?"

In fact, he'd pretty much decided to do just that. But he wasn't going to announce it now. This was Brett and Haley's day. "It's still under consideration."

Brett elbowed him. "You could be closer to the family. And I'm sure Carly would love it if Uncle Sean dropped by to baby-sit every Friday night."

"You know, you're making that decision easier by the minute," Sean warned good-naturedly. "Another Denver winter is starting to look good."

His older sister, Isabel, wandered over, sipping a slender-stemmed glass of champagne. She glanced at the cans in their hands. "Beer?" She shook her head in disgust. "And we had such high hopes that a college degree would bring some element of civilization to you both."

"Where do you think we perfected our beer-drinking skills in the first place?" Sean asked.

"Champagne is for sissies, Iz," Brett added, sipping with exaggeration from his already empty can, then belching just to disgust his sister. Worked every time.

Sean contributed his share, just because he could.

Isabel sighed in resignation. "Well, it didn't seem too much like a sissy drink earlier when you were making that toast."

Sean grinned. "Yeah, but it's a lot more manly when you're sipping it from the maid of honor's satin high heel."

She shook her head. "Men."

Brett caught Sean's eye, then glanced down meaningfully at their empty beer cans. Sean chuckled. At exactly the same moment, they crushed the beer cans on their foreheads.

"Oh, jeez!" She quickly shifted so the rest of the gathering wouldn't see them, protecting her brothers even as it was clear she'd just as soon throttle them both. "Don't let Haley see you do 'frat boy' stunts. She can still get an annulment, you know." She shot a look at Sean. "And don't say a word. You're a lost cause anyway."

"You're one to talk," Sean countered, but she was already waltzing off. She did that particular exit very well. Much more effective than Carly's standard stalk-off-in-a-huff. But then, Izzy'd had plenty of practice. Just ask any man she'd dated more than three times.

"Uh-oh," Sean said as he surveyed the reception scene. "Uncle Padraig just grabbed his fiddle. You might want to save Haley before—"

"Don't worry," Brett reassured him with a smug smile. "She actually finds us charming."

Sean just shot him a look. "Maybe she should get her head examined. That earthquake you two got tangled up in obviously harmed her more seriously than you thought."

Brett just laughed as he headed across the lawn and swept his bride into a jig.

Sean thought about Haley's family, none of whom had made the trip from their snooty east coast enclave to the banks of the Bayou Duplantier to see their only daughter marry beneath herself. He raised his crushed beer can to their absence. "Your loss," he murmured, then slapped his thighs, and Recon, Brett's rescue-trained dog, and Digger, Haley's little Jack Russell terror, trotted over to him.

He looked down at the two of them and snorted. "Yellow bows? Whose idea was it to stick bows on your ears?" Carly's probably. "Don't you know all your dog friends will laugh behind your backs?" They just looked up at him, tongues lolling, eyes bright. He smiled. "But, hey, they got me into this monkey suit. So who am I to throw stones, eh?"

At the word "throw" Recon's ears perked. Sean looked around, found a decent stick and hurled it down the rear hill of the Gannon property, then followed the two dogs as they raced to the edge of the river that chugged slowly by.

Loss. Marriage. The two words echoed in his mind as he watched Digger wrestle the stick away from Recon. The little dog was admirably confident against the bigger and very well-muscled Labrador—who immediately let him have the prize. "Women," he said to Recon, who was female despite her macho moniker. "Why is it you feel compelled to let the guy win?" He grabbed the stick from Digger and threw it again. "Do you really think our egos are so fragile?" He looked up the hill at Brett, who was gingerly holding the baby a beaming Carly had just placed in his arms, and grinned. "More likely you're just tricking us into believing we really stand a fighting chance."

His smile faded as he continued to wander the edge of the property, uncomfortable with the direction his thoughts were heading. Introspection—at least about big life issues such as marriage, everlasting love and raising a family—was something in which U.S. Deputy Marshal Sean Gannon simply didn't indulge.

It surprised him that Brett's wedding had done something as clichéd as make him think about his own life. When his sister Carly had married two years ago he had wished her well and been thankful as hell to get back on that plane to Denver.

Now? Maybe it was the danger both Brett and Haley had been in when they'd met up again in California and his realizing how close he'd come to losing his brother. How close his brother had come to losing his future wife. That was enough to make anyone rethink what was important. And though they drove him crazy, family was important to Sean. Important enough that he'd all but put in the transfer to the full-time, stationary position of trainer for the Marshals' Special Ops team right here in Louisiana.

Of course, he hadn't totally lost his mind. He was still a long way from seeing himself involved in a serious relationship, much less engaged, married or reproducing. But as the excited squeal of some of the Gannon cousins' kids filled the muggy early evening air, he was forced to admit that, at the same time, he wasn't exactly where he'd thought he'd be at this stage in his life. He'd surpassed his career goals a long time ago, but somehow he'd never figured out how to work in the wife-and-family part he'd been certain he'd have by now. Not that he'd wasted a lot of time worrying about it. Or any time, really. He'd always been too damn busy to worry about anything but his next assignment.

Which, of course, was exactly why he found himself in his present situation at this stage of his life. Highly trained, very successful, financially secure...and alone.

Recon trotted over and dropped the stick at his feet. He rubbed her head. "Ah, a loyal woman," he told her, tossing the stick again. The Labrador looked at the stick, glanced up the yard to where Digger was begging food from one of the endless number of aunts and uncles, and promptly left the stick where it lay—not interested if Digger didn't want to play.

"That's a man for you, Recon," he told her. "Always looking for the better handout. You're better off taking care of yourself. That way you'll never be disappointed."

Panting, she stared up at him with those liquid brown eyes then turned and trotted back, snagged the stick and loped back up the hill. Sean watched as she sauntered by Digger, flashing the stick, then racing off around the buffet table. Digger took one last longing look at Aunt Miranda's chicken wing, then went tearing off after Recon.

Sean hooted with laughter. "Well, I guess that's my problem right there. I've never met the woman who wants me bad enough to keep waving her treasure under my nose when I get sidetracked by something else."

Which was probably the closest he'd come to admitting his real problem where settling down was concerned. He always believed the right woman would come along and he'd just know it, and the rest would simply fall into place.

In the meantime he wasn't averse to short-lived, very hot interludes. But he'd gotten so wrapped up in work lately that what little personal life he had had fallen by the wayside. Which had him thinking about his next assignment. Most men would kill for it. He was to deliver some documents and set up meetings with the head deputy in St. Thomas in the U.S. Virgin Islands. Five days of long meetings...but six nights of nothing to do but enjoy island life. He'd earned the assignment; he knew that. And it was pathetic to admit, but he was somewhat at a loss as to what he was going to do with those long nights.

Digger trotted up to him then, stick firmly clamped in his little jaws. Recon stood behind him, wagging her tail.

"Yeah, yeah, I hear ya," he said with a shake of his head and a grin. "I'll just make sure to pack my trusty stick."

NINTH JUDICIAL COURT Judge Laurel Patrick stared at the plane ticket in her hand and smiled. She should be upset at her father's underhanded tactics. But Seamus Patrick knew how to get what he wanted, had learned that skill even before being elected to the Louisiana supreme court bench nine years earlier. Any other time she'd have privately snarled at him for using the annual Christmas party at *her* courthouse as a platform for announcing his present to her. Of course, it had been *his* courthouse long before it had ever been hers. Not that it was solely hers now, of course.

She was one of a number of justices that heard cases in the Alexandria parish courtrooms. But she was part of the Patrick judicial dynasty, started in the United States by her great-grandfather, Donal, the first Patrick raised in this country, although originally established by several Patricks before him back on the bonny shores of Ireland. So it helped if she carved out her own spot, even if it was just in her own mind.

Naturally, Seamus Patrick didn't understand her need to carve her own niche. If he had, she wouldn't be a justice. Hell, she wouldn't even have been a lawyer. But she hadn't had the nerve as a child, much less as a teenager heading off, scholarship in hand, to the college of her choice, to tell her father, or her grandfather, that the footsteps she really wanted to follow were those of her mother. And her grandmother before her. That of being a wife, raising children, making a home for them. She'd dreamed of that, of becoming involved in the community, in her church, as the women in her family had a long tradition of doing.

All of which would have been a fine, even admirable, goal...if she'd had any brothers. Or even any sisters with a thirst for law. But she hadn't. It had just been her. The last Patrick of the famous—though some would say infamous—Justice Patricks. The only one left to carry on the tradition. Skipping a generation to await any potential future justices she might procreate was simply not an option.

She glanced at the brochure that had come with the plane ticket, still stunned by the gift. Four Days In Paradise, it shouted in hot-pink letters. Underneath was a photo of a white sandy beach and crystalline-blue water.

But what Laurel saw was escape. Four days away from work that had, of late, caused a headache that wouldn't cease, a stomach lining that a fistful antacids could no longer calm, circles under her eyes that makeup no longer completely covered, a complexion made sallow from too many nights pouring over filings, motions and briefs, and not enough time spent out in the real world having what other people called a life.

"It's a wonder Alan wants me at all," she murmured. She gritted her teeth against the burning sensation in her gut that just the thought of him brought on. Why in the hell was he being so persistent? she wondered for the umpteenth time. And, for the umpteenth time, she didn't have an answer.

But what she did have was a plane ticket away from the bench...and away from Alan Bentley's increasingly annoying and very unwanted attentions.

Her father made his way through the throng of

party revelers and tucked her against his side with one beefy arm. At the towering height of six foot five, Seamus was intimidating enough without his booming Irish voice and stern visage, both of which he used to great advantage in all avenues of his life.

Despite the fact that Laurel had never been as passionate as he had been about the legal life they pursued, she did take great pride in her accomplishments, her stellar record and even the comparisons people made between father and daughter. Of course, he could still make her feel like a seven-year-old looking for his approval by memorizing all the liability torts in one of his ground-breaking civil suits with nothing more than a certain look...or an arm around the shoulder.

Any other time she might have pulled away...with a smile and a affectionate dig at his orchestrations. But he'd honestly stunned her with his gift. Had he seen the telltale signs of the stress she was under? Had he suspected she needed a break, a chance to get a grip on a life that suddenly felt as though it was spiraling out of control? It wasn't unreasonable to think so. For all that he'd railroaded her into her career, he'd done so with a deep love and honest affection that was hard to thwart and an unfailing confidence in her that had carried her through many a long night, both in law school, during her years as an assistant district attorney, and even now, on the bench.

His gift had made her wonder if maybe she'd been wrong in keeping her escalating problems to herself. Right at that moment she wanted nothing more than to curl into his strength, his warmth, his security, and tell him everything. Tell him how concerned she was about her constant fatigue, about the emotional toll adjudicating cases was taking on her. How she respected the honor of her position, but wasn't sure she wanted to continue on the bench.

How she was being all but stalked by the current district attorney.

"Hard feelings?" her father asked. "Don't be cross with me. I knew if I'd done it in private, you'd have tossed that ticket right back in my face."

How right he was, too. And it was because he was too often right—annoyingly so—she found the strength to pull away from him to deliver her best Judge Patrick look.

Her father merely raised his bushy eyebrows in anticipation.

"No hard feelings," she said. "But you'll want to remember three things." She ticked them off. "One, the apple didn't fall far from the tree. Two, I know when your birthday is and that you'll be hitting the big seven-oh." She smiled a smile that only a newly minted defense attorney would mistake as friendly—and then, only once. "Three, paybacks are hell when delivered by other people. But when delivered by a Patrick, there is no time off for good behavior."

Seamus tipped his head back and roared with laughter, another trademark—and one often heard echoing throughout his chambers. "I wish your mother was here to see what a fine lass she brought into this world."

"Are you kidding? Mom would be horrified to know how deeply you've corrupted her only child."

Seamus and Laurel both smiled, as they always did when the subject of Alena Patrick came up. "She knew you were never going to be a princess."

Laurel sighed. "I know. I'm beginning to think she was smarter than both of us put together."

Seamus's smile faded, replaced by the look of concern Laurel had hoped to avoid. "Is everything okay?" he asked. "Is the upcoming Rochambeau case giving you a hard time, because we both know Jack Rochambeau is a horse's—"

"Yes," Laurel broke in, once again smiling. "As does the entire legal community. But he comes from a long line of them, many of them dangerous, so he's gotten away with it. But if the D.A.'s case is as strong as it's purported to be, that's about to come to an end."

"That's my girl."

"Maybe you could give the rest of his 'family' these tickets, though. Now *that* would make my life a lot easier." She waved the resort brochure.

Seamus smiled, but the concern didn't leave his brilliant blue eyes. "I know things have been rough lately, Laurel. That you've landed more than your fair share of difficult cases. And now this one."

"You always said it was the benchmark cases that made a career. This one definitely qualifies."

"Yes, but I believe I also said that a career was only worth the people who benefited from it."

Stung, she said, "I think you can safely say more than a few people have benefited from my rulings. And it goes without saying that any damage we can do to organized crime scum like the Rochambeaus—"

"Laurel, I don't mean the victims and their families. I'm talking about *your* family."

"But you're my family. My only—"

"Besides me."

"There is no one besides you."

"Precisely."

Laurel sighed and remembered why she didn't discuss her personal life with her father. Even when she was having one, which she wasn't at present. "Dad, I do not want to hear the 'biological clock' lecture again. Being a judge makes it difficult to have—"

"Absolutely it does," he broke in, as he always did. "And your mother was a saint and an angel for putting up with me. And you, for that matter," he added with his charming smile. She didn't fall for it. But then, she was more immune than most.

"You groomed me for this since the first time Mom used your law books as my booster seat," Laurel reminded him. She might have followed in her father's famous footsteps, but that didn't mean she didn't tug on the strings every once in a while. Too much Seamus in her not to. "So don't complain I'm not popping out grandchildren for you to terrorize."

"Terrorize is it now? Is that what you think I did to you?"

He was teasing, but she was too fatigued to play along. So she did the one thing guaranteed to end any argument she no longer had the stamina to continue. She didn't resort to it often, mostly because it went right to his head. She stepped in and hugged him, pressed a kiss to his cheek and whispered, "I'm proud to be your daughter."

"Ah, sweetheart," he sighed, squeezing her.

She'd have felt guilty, except she'd only spoken the truth. She *was* proud to be his daughter. And, truth be told, she'd followed in his footsteps as much to find out what it felt like to be even a tiny bit like him, as she had to make him proud of her. From day one he'd made the legal world seem like a thrilling classroom with endless boundaries begging to be explored. He'd also made her feel that she was incredibly lucky to be the student who could do that exploring. And she'd been a good student. A very good student. Good enough that, over time, she'd begun to believe that succeeding in the legal field was enough. And having his respect was proof she'd made the right choice.

"I'd give you a dozen grandbabies if I could," she told him. "But we don't always get to have it all." She stepped back, feeling more than a little twinge when she saw the flicker of pain in his eyes as he thought of his beloved wife, her mother. She'd been gone for seven years now, yet there wasn't a day that went by that they both didn't still miss her. "And you never know," she added, wishing now she'd opted for his lecture. "Maybe I'll meet some island man, fall hopelessly in love and drag him back to Louisiana with me. Where I'll force him to be my house husband and rear a whole pack of squalling Patricks."

Seamus's smile blinked back on and she sighed a little in relief.

He leaned in and pecked her on the cheek. "You know I love you."

She sighed a little and blinked back the sudden moisture that burned at the backs of her eyes. "I love you, too, Dad."

He tapped the ticket still clutched in her hand. "Enjoy this," he instructed, once again Justice Patrick. "Use the time wisely. Leave the work here. Lord knows it's not going anywhere." He squeezed her elbow, then motioned to one of the court clerks who was trying to get his attention. He looked back down at her and winked. "And if you meet that beach bum, make sure he signs a prenup."

Laurel's mouth dropped open, but she laughed as her father disappeared in the crowd. A fling with a beach bum. Maybe that's just what she needed. "Yeah, and the best thing about an island fling is he can't resurface almost a year later, begging to be back in my life."

She tapped the brochure against her palm, then tucked it in her suit pocket as a plan began to form. She'd leave a note for Alan, explaining—again—but this time with as much finality as she could muster, that there would be no getting back together. Then she would leave town for a while, let it sink in, give him time to come to terms with it.

Before they squared off again in her courtroom.

Four days to rejuvenate. To languish. To read a book. Get some sun. Drink something with an umbrella in it. "And maybe get laid," she said, a grin curving her lips.

"Excuse me?" the young clerk next to her said.

She hadn't realized she'd spoken out loud and quickly said, "It's getting late." She waved her brochure and grinned, the first from-the-heart grin she'd felt in ages. "I have a plane to catch."

2

"ARE YOU GOING to the bonfire tonight? Did I mention your hotel puts on a nice beach party?"

"Yes, you did," Sean replied. *Several times.* He shook his head as he held the door for Trenton Warner, the head deputy of the Virgin Islands Marshals Office in St. Thomas. "But I don't think so."

Trent looked crestfallen. But then, he hadn't been exactly subtle in his efforts to set Sean up with some extracurricular activities. "Come now, all work and no play—"

Sean laughed. "I didn't say I wasn't going to play. Just that I wasn't planning on doing it at a hotel beach party." He'd been put up in a nice little hotel on Morning Star Bay, a bit of a distance from Charlotte Amalie, the capital city of St. Thomas. And the place was definitely teeming with scantily clad women. Except for the fact that they were a tad bit too...well, nubile, for his taste. Which was likely exactly why Trent had booked him there. Even though Sean was only thirty-four, gazing down from his balcony at all that tanned, oiled skin on women barely old enough to vote, made him feel...well, old.

"Whatever you say," Trent said with a sigh and a shake of his head. "And here I was hoping to live vicariously through you." He was fifty-five, married, with two sons currently enrolled at Florida State.

"What good is staying single for so long if you're not going to take advantage of it?"

"I imagine there are places other than that beach shindig to find a little company," Sean responded, though he hadn't the first clue where that might be and, in truth, had no real plans in place to find out.

"Ah, sly devil." Trent laughed and nudged him in the side. "You've probably already hooked up with someone. What, did you meet her on the plane? Or in the airport this morning on your way in?"

"No, I haven't 'hooked up.'" And yet he couldn't deny that the balmy air and white sandy stretch of beach had made him feel a bit...needy.

"Sure, sure. You just don't want an audience," Trent goaded. "A little island-magic-just-for-two. I get it."

Sean flashed a grin. "I don't mind an audience. Just don't care for sand in my britches."

Trent hooted then slapped him on the back as Sean opened the door of his rental Jeep. "Well, whatever the hell you have planned, you have a good time doing it. And if you're looking for a good meal to bolster the stamina, give Sam's a try. It's past your hotel about a mile or so, right on the water. The snapper is incredible."

"Thanks for the tip. I'll catch you in the morning."

"Nine sharp." Trent sent him a mock salute. "Don't do anything I wouldn't do. But by all means do everything I'd like to do but can't."

Sean just snorted. "Hey, I saw that picture of your wife on your desk. I'm not feeling all that sorry for you." He waved as he pulled out, leaving Trent laughing but nodding in agreement. Sean smiled, thinking Mrs. Warner was probably going to have a very good night.

He drove back to the hotel, wondering what it was like to head home to the same woman night after night, for years on end. Hell, he wondered what it was like to head home to any woman, any night, period. He used his job, and the dedication and time he put into it, as his reason—excuse, really—for remaining single. But if he was honest with himself, he'd have to admit it went beyond that. He was so used to being captain of his own domain, doing what he wanted, when he wanted. When it came right down to it, he couldn't imagine adjusting his lifestyle to include the wants and needs of another person.

He sighed and shifted his attention to the stunning island scenery. Maybe he simply wasn't cut out for marriage. Considering the huge family he'd come from, it pained him to even think that, much less imagine telling his parents. Yet the evidence was piling up, the years were passing by. He felt a little twist in his gut at the notion of never having kids. But you sort of had to have the relationship and the wife to get to the rest, didn't you?

Well, wife and kids or no, he sure as hell wasn't planning on entering a monastery anytime soon, either. And while he hadn't had much time to devote to extracurricular activities of late, he sure had some time now.

A whole week of it. Starting right now. He gripped the steering wheel a bit harder as he took the curving island road toward his hotel. So where in the hell did he begin? He'd apparently missed out on the airport love connection. Which left him with island social life. But he was too old to pick up chicks in bars. Not that he'd ever been all that keen on the bar-hopping and club-cruising scene, even when he'd been young and stupid. Which left...what? He snorted. "Call girls... and bonfire bunnies." He wasn't entirely sure which option scared him more.

"You're a pathetic excuse for a bachelor, you know that?" Christ, he was still young, and although women's tongues probably didn't hang out when he walked by, he didn't think he was too hard on the eyes. His body was in pretty damn good shape, thanks to all that Special Ops training. He wasn't rich, but living alone hadn't left him exactly hurting financially. *And yet you can't figure out how to get laid to save your life*, he thought in disgust.

He slowed the Jeep as he neared the hotel entrance. Situated on a little jut of land, the hotel was not exactly remote, but not sandwiched in the middle of a cluster of other hotels or tourist traps, either. Off the beaten track. Like his love life of late, he thought with a dry smile.

Best of all, his room was on the top floor of the four-story building. It boasted a stunning view of Hassel and Water islands rising up from the clear blue of the water out past the harbor and the mountains bumping up behind the curve of the shoreline on the opposite side of the bay. He'd run the beach this morning as the sun had edged the horizon and thought he could definitely get used to such a daily routine. Living in Denver, his view was usually of mountain roads and snow-crusted peaks. He'd enjoyed his years stationed there, but he had to admit that the warmth of the sun was a welcome change. Reminded him of Louisiana. Of home.

He glanced up at the hotel, then down at the cluster

of white-clad hotel staffers, dotting the beach, busily preparing for the evening's festivities...and pressed the gas pedal. He drove past the parking lot and continued on down the coast road, out toward the east end of the island. He passed Sam's, thinking maybe he'd take a long evening drive, come back for a nice fish dinner, then run the beach as the sun set. Be back in his room before the party began. Shower, sit on the balcony with a beer, put on that suspense thriller he'd picked up at the airport and listen to the festivities and music below while he relaxed. All in all, not a bad evening. Even if there wasn't going to be any sex involved. Sex was great, but certainly a man could manage to survive—

Sean hit the brakes as he rounded a bend and swerved away from a woman pushing a small Vespa motor scooter along the edge of the road.

She was wearing snug navy pants that ended just below the knee, spanking-white sneakers and a loose white T-shirt knotted on one hip. Tendrils of dark hair had escaped her loose ponytail to cling to her cheeks and neck. Her face was flushed and her white cotton shirt clung to her back. Just how far had she pushed that thing?

Sean immediately tugged the steering wheel and pulled off the road. When she darted him a suspicious glance, he realized that his Good Samaritan act might not be so interpreted by a woman alone on a quiet stretch of road. So, along with a smile, he pulled out his wallet. The one with his badge tucked inside.

"Hey, there," he called as he got out of the Jeep and flipped open his wallet. "Do you need some help? Sean Gannon, Deputy U.S. Marshal." His smile widened as she paused. "In case you thought I was the St. Thomas stalker or something."

He'd expected... Well, he didn't know. Some flash of humor or even exasperation at his lame attempt at charm. He hadn't expected the real flash of... Fear was too strong a word. But she'd definitely tensed up a bit at the term "stalker."

"Is there one?" she asked, finally finding an amused smile. Her voice was smooth, a bit melodic...almost familiar-sounding.

"One what?" he asked distractedly. Then his brain clicked into gear. Damn, he really did have to get out more. "Oh, no, there isn't. I just didn't want you to be alarmed."

She leaned the motor scooter against her thigh and turned to face him more fully. "You have an odd way of putting a woman at ease."

"It really has been too long, then," he murmured more to himself than her.

"Since what?" she asked.

He evaded answering that by saying, "Something tells me you'd hold up just fine, even if I wasn't a Good Samaritan."

She smiled fully then, and he found himself wishing she'd take those dark sunglasses off so he could see her eyes.

She nodded at the wallet he was still holding out. "So, Deputy Gannon. You here on business?"

"Yes, ma'am." And listening to her, he finally realized why she seemed familiar to him. "What makes you think I'm visiting, though? We have offices here on the island."

She nodded at his Jeep. "Rental." She smiled again

when he nodded in appreciation of her deduction. "Nice tan, though."

He chuckled. "Actually, I just got here. That's from sun glare off the snow back in Denver."

"And you were forced to leave the cold and the snow to come here. Tough assignment."

"Yeah, it's hard work." He grinned. "But they let me out nights."

"Which you spend rescuing damsels in distress. Don't you know how to take time off?"

"Are you asking because you also need help in that department?"

She looked surprised. "What do you mean? For all you know, I spend all my time scootering around exotic islands."

He gestured to her scooter. "Rental."

She fought a smile. "So?" she challenged. "Maybe I don't like the burden of ownership."

He pointed to her blindingly white shoes. "Your sneakers...brand new."

"Maybe I'm obsessive about dirt."

He nodded in appreciation of her savvy defense. A shame it wasn't going to hold up. "And you have a tag. Hanging from the back of your shirt."

She reflexively reached behind her and the scooter swerved around her leg, about to roll to its side.

Sean closed the distance between them in two long strides and grabbed the Vespa before it could hit the ground. "Sorry," he said sincerely, tugging the scooter away from her and balancing it upright again. "I should have just said 'it takes one to know one' and left it at that. I didn't mean to embarrass you."

She eyed him closely—at least as best as he could

tell through those large, dark lenses. "I almost believe you mean that," she said.

He laughed. "How else did you think I pegged you?"

"Because you're trained to be astutely observant?"

He laughed, enjoying her quick wit. "Oh, absolutely. That and the fact that, other than the official attire you see right now, everything else I have to wear while I'm here was bought either in the Denver airport or in the hotel lobby this morning. I probably have the receipts on me somewhere."

Now she flashed another smile. "I guess flowered shirts and bathing suits aren't necessary in Colorado."

He looked at her in mock disbelief. "How did you know I favor tacky island wear? What gave me away?"

She laughed and he felt... He couldn't put a name to it. Freer?

"Just a guess," she countered. "Although, to be honest, you look more like a faded-sweatpants-and-ancient-college-T-shirt kind of guy."

He grinned. He'd jogged in that exact ensemble this morning. "You win."

"My father would be so proud."

"Is he back home in Louisiana, I hope?" He lifted a hand as she stiffened and backed away. "It was the accent that gave you away. I have family in Baton Rouge." He let the South back into his voice as he said it.

"Ah."

She didn't offer any additional comment and Sean spent a moment casting about for something else to say. Then he just came out and asked what he really wanted to know. "So, are you here with family?" Not as clumsy as blurting that he wanted to know if she was married, but it ran a close second.

"No," she said, but once again didn't elaborate. "You?" she asked after a moment.

"No. I'm solo. Here and in Denver." Oh, great, how desperate and pathetic did that sound? But, if anything was going to happen—and he'd be a fool to say no, right?—well, he didn't want any misunderstandings. So he braved it out. "You?"

She lifted a shoulder in a half shrug, as if it wasn't of any consequence to her. "Solo. By choice."

"Obviously," he said with an appreciative smile, then winced when she merely rolled her eyes. "Too strong, huh? I'm a bit out of practice."

That got a small snort out of her, which made him laugh.

"Honest," he told her. "The workaholic thing. Makes dating and relationships a bit tough."

"So you don't make it down to the island office often then."

"This would be the inaugural time, yes."

"Hmm," she said.

They both drifted into a short silence while Sean tried to come up with something clever and witty and unmoronic to say. It might have been a while since he'd done the verbal tango with a woman, but he usually wasn't this rusty. "I'd be glad to take you and your scooter wherever you'd like to go."

"Actually, I was only planning to push it until I came upon a place with a phone. The resort can come and get both me and this death trap." She sent the bright yellow scooter a fulminating look.

"You two not getting along?"

She shifted the look to him.

He grinned. "I thought maybe you'd just run out of gas."

"What I've run out of is enthusiasm for forced frolic." She sighed. "I'm sorry. That sounds ungrateful and whiny. And though I'm feeling more than a little of both at the moment, neither is directed at you. I appreciate the offer of help. If you have a cell phone, I'd be in your debt if you'd allow me to use it to place a call."

"Why don't we pile this in the back of my Jeep and go find someplace that serves cold drinks and a hot meal? Then I'll take you both to your hotel." He lifted a hand when she began to protest. "It will allow me to meet my Good Samaritan quota for the day and it will keep you from committing scooter-cide."

She laughed despite herself. "You have a point. I've listened to a lot of debate on the death penalty, but this is the first time I've considered administering it myself."

"You haven't listened to my dinner conversation yet."

Her smile remained. "I'll consider that fair warning."

"Are you accepting then?"

She shifted her weight and he just knew she was going to turn him down. Hell, considering how dorky he was acting, he'd turn himself down. You'd think he'd never flirted with a beautiful woman before. Something about her though...just left him tongue-tied.

She paused just long enough in answering that he suspected she might actually want to say yes despite whatever reservations she had. He was surprised at how badly he wanted to sway her to a yes. Even more surprising was that he wanted her company and yet wasn't already picturing them naked and sweaty. In fact, he doubted very seriously this would lead to anything of the sort. It was clear she wasn't the one-night-stand type. And, frankly, a few brief flings aside, neither was he. Or he would have hit the bonfire.

But, at the moment, an attractive companion who would make dinner a lively and fun occasion sounded pretty good. And if there was a little spike of sexual tension to go along with it...well, he wasn't going to quibble.

"Did you have other plans for dinner? Or did the Scooter of Death ruin that, too?"

"No," she said. "No plans."

"Then say yes."

Her lips parted slightly in surprise. Maybe he'd said that a bit more commandingly than he'd intended.

"Please," he added with what he hoped was a winning smile. Brett was the Gannon who'd been blessed with all the easy charm, although Clay ran a close second. Sean had always been a bit more serious by nature, had always had to work at the charming part.

"Would it be asking too much to head to where I'm staying first?" she asked.

He could have told her he'd take her to the moon and back first if she'd agree to dinner.

"I'd just like the chance to change. I'm a little—"

She broke off when Sean reached out. She instinctively pulled back, but he reached anyway...and tugged the tag off the back of her shirt. "There. Now you look perfect."

"Oh, you're such a liar. But my ego thanks you." She shook her head and laughed a little as she contemplated what she was about to do. "I really shouldn't do this."

"Give me one good reason why we shouldn't rescue each other from our own inability to relax. We'll force each other to sit and watch the world go by without being active participants in it for a whole hour or two."

"Just one good reason?"

"What, you have a list? Am I handling this that terribly?"

Her laugh was fuller this time. "Just badly enough to be endearing and to make me less self-conscious."

"Thanks. I think."

She smiled. "You just strike me as someone who is way too used to getting his own way."

"Oh?"

"Rusty flirting skills notwithstanding, you have this...commanding way about you."

Any other woman would have said that and it would have sounded suggestive as hell. Not with her. She'd simply sounded...honest. Maybe it was the quirky way her brows furrowed when she said it, as if she couldn't quite decide if she liked commanding, rusty flirts or not.

So why his body reacted the way it did...he couldn't say. *Dinner*. This was just about dinner.

"I take it you don't respond well to commands," he said when she let the silence spin out. He shoved his hands into his pockets. Mostly because he had this absurd need to reach out and snatch her sunglasses off to get a better look at her eyes...and what was going on behind those glasses. "What about a humble request?"

She laughed lightly. "Somehow I'm thinking you didn't make it into the Marshals Service by being humble and unprepossessing."

"I didn't say anything about being unprepossessing." He slid his hands out, then shifted a little as he realized the fit of his trousers was being compromised by more than just his hands stretching the confines of his pockets. "Just a nice simple rescue and dinner."

"And if I just want to be rescued?"

"I'll be forced to eat alone, which probably means I'll end up working to pass the time."

"Ah, so now I would be doing you a favor in return for helping me get rid of this junk heap. And given as how I'm not all that keen on finding myself in need of rescue in the first place, this does make your case stronger."

"If you decide against me, is there any hope for an appeal?"

She grinned. "Oh, I think you have a very good case for appeal."

His grin widened. Maybe charm came more easily with the right inspiration. "Do I?"

She smiled, lifting her shoulders in a helpless shrug. "The court finds in your favor, Deputy Marshal Gannon. You are awarded one dinner—in which both parties will make equal payment," she added with emphasis. "And a rescue, to take place prior to said meal." She lifted a finger when he began to argue. "You've already pleaded your case. In exchange for the rescue, you will be prevented from overwork and exhaustion, which should be against the law anyway in such a gorgeous tropical setting."

"Thank you, Justice—?"

She stuck out her hand, her smile a bit smug now. "Justice Laurel Patrick, of the Ninth Judicial Court of Alexandria Parish."

"And here I was only kidding."

She sighed lightly. "Sometimes I wish I was."

But before he could ask her to follow up on that interesting little comment, she had taken the Vespa by the handlebars and was rolling it toward the rear of his Jeep.

He managed to haul it into the open back and wedge it, albeit somewhat awkwardly, in between the rear spare tire and front seat back. He motioned to the passenger side. "I'd open your door for you...but there isn't one." He'd never owned a Jeep before and was definitely enjoying the free feel of it. Having her beside him would just make it perfect. Which was when it struck him that, for the first time in he couldn't remember how long, he was actually enjoying himself. And it had nothing whatsoever to do with work.

She got in as he slid back behind the wheel.

"Where to?" he asked.

She didn't speak for a moment, then shook her head and, very quietly, almost too quietly for him to hear, said, "The Resort."

He looked at her. "The Resort. As in...*The* Resort? The private club out on Flamingo Cay?"

"In my own defense, I didn't pick it. My father did."

"Your *father*? I have to meet this guy."

"No. You don't."

She'd said it so emphatically, he had to laugh. "You're only making me more curious, you know."

She sighed. "He knew I needed a break. He probably had no idea about the resort's...reputation. Neither did I, until I got here. The brochure looked totally tame."

The Resort sat just off the south shore of St. Thomas on its own tiny spit of land. It was one of those private, all-inclusive clubs, like they had in Jamaica or Mexico, where certain rules of decorum were a bit more...relaxed. In this case, extremely relaxed, at least if the local island ads he'd spied in the morning paper were anything to go by.

He glanced at her and decided he didn't want to risk losing his dinner companion. So he let the titillating subject of Flamingo Cay drop. For now, anyway. "Do you like seafood?"

"What?"

"Seafood? Stuff caught under water and cooked up for people to eat."

She shot him a long-suffering look, which for some reason made him grin all the wider. "Yes, as it happens, I do. As long as someone else does the catching." She wrinkled her nose. "And, for that matter, the cooking."

"Fine, then we'll go and ditch the Scooter of Death and head to a little place I heard about back closer to Charlotte Amalie." He was already heading down the coast road as he spoke.

"Why do I get the feeling that I lost complete control the moment I got into this Jeep?"

Sean laughed. "I don't know. Maybe the same reason that I feel like I lost all control the moment I swerved around that bend in the road...and found you."

3

LAUREL LET THE WARM, early evening wind snatch and tug at her ponytail...and tried not to think too much about what she'd just agreed to do. A woman alone on an exotic island had no business standing on the side of the road talking to—okay, flirting with—a strange man...much less getting into his vehicle and riding off with him!

He's a deputy marshal, for God's sake, she reminded herself. He was hardly going to attack her. *Yeah, but he's still a man.* And she knew quite well just how capable they were of causing a great deal of trouble, no matter their job description.

She shook that train of thought from her head. She'd given Alan far too much of her precious time back at home. She'd be damned if she'd let him ruin any part of her precious break. Break. She squelched the urge to laugh. So far she'd been on the island a grand total of twenty-four hours and this was the first time she'd felt remotely relaxed.

She'd wandered down to the pool just after checking in, but the sight of all that young, fit, taut and mostly naked skin—and dear Lord but there had been a never-ending sea of it—had dampened her enthusiasm for revealing her pasty-white, bench-sitting, thirty-two-year-old body. She'd spent her first evening in her room, sitting on her balcony with a glass of chilled wine, trying to pay more attention to the setting sun than to the somewhat startling goings-on in the club below. She didn't consider herself a prude by any means but, for heaven's sake, the nightclub in the center of the resort resembled something more of a Greek orgy than the open-air dance floor the brochure had purported it to be.

But not to be daunted, this morning she'd gamely pulled on her newly purchased vacation clothes and taken the water taxi over to the mainland, deciding to rent a scooter to see some of the island. *And we all know how well that went*, she thought wryly. From the engine conking out when she was miles from anywhere, to leaving the tags on her shirt, one would think she needed a keeper.

She skimmed a glance sideways, then hid the private little smile. Okay, so things were looking up. But she wasn't sure, despite the badge and his claim to being a workaholic, that having Sean Gannon as her keeper was going to prevent her from getting into any more trouble. In fact, he made her think about all kinds of trouble she could get into. If she let herself go there. Which, of course, she would not.

It was just a nice dinner. And that alone was a heck of a lot better than the evening she'd envisioned just an hour earlier. Which had basically involved making it back to the resort, on her knees if necessary, showering off the road dust and sweat, then collapsing facedown on her bed. With maybe a room service meal later on, if she revived herself in time.

Dinner with the deputy was definitely a step up. Not that she planned on sharing that particular sentiment with him.

He wasn't the kind of man one encouraged. He was

quite bold enough as it was, without any provocation from her. Though for some reason she couldn't quite name, he'd managed to provoke her a deal more than most men. It's only dinner, she reminded herself yet again, firmly shutting out images of what she could be doing back on Flamingo Cay with a man like Sean Gannon. Suddenly the club's atmosphere seemed a lot less sleazy...and a lot more sensual.

Not that she'd ever encourage that kind of lascivious behavior. Because, after all, she was a judge. And a Patrick. If her father knew where he'd sent her, he'd surely be horrified. At least she hoped he would be. So dinner it was. And nothing more would come of it, although just the realization that something more might made her body zing.

It had been a long time since she'd had zing. A really long time.

Sean turned at the sign indicating The Resort's water ferry dock and Laurel shut out any and all trailing thoughts about Sean and Flamingo Cay...and zing.

"Everything okay?" Sean asked. "That was quite a sigh," he added when she looked at him questioningly.

"Oh," she replied. "I'm sorry. It wasn't the company. Promise."

He still looked concerned. "Just how far did you have to push that thing anyway?"

"Not all that far." It had felt like a million miles. On the surface of the sun. "I'd love a quick shower, though, if you don't mind."

The moment the words left her mouth, she saw the potential suggestiveness of her request register on Sean's face. To his credit, he didn't respond to it. Which only made her envision exactly what it would be like to take a shower...with Sean. His face was all hard, tanned angles made more prominent by his almost brutally short haircut. His eyes were dark and they flashed dangerously when he smiled. His teeth were sharply straight and white, set between lips that looked as hard and chiseled as his face...that she bet felt anything but when pressed to someone's soft skin—

His expression began to change and she vaguely realized he'd been staring at her as she'd fantasized about him. She jerked her gaze toward the water ferry. "I'm supposed to turn the scooter in here. They have depots all over the island, but the guy that rented it to me back in Charlotte Amalie said there was one right by The Resort's ferry dock and—" She stopped, abruptly aware she was babbling to cover the sudden spike of sexual tension arcing—no, zinging—between them. And, God help her, the man gave very good zing.

To his further credit, when he smiled, it wasn't smug or knowing. But then, it didn't have to be. Neither of them could possibly deny the heat blossoming between them inside the tiny confines of the Jeep. And convertible or not, at the moment it felt downright intimate.

"I believe the depot is there," he said in that flat uninflected tone he had. He motioned behind her.

But she didn't follow the gesture. She was too busy wondering if it was the marshal's training that had taken the South out of his voice, or just time spent away from home. When the drawl had crept into his voice earlier, even for those few words, the effect had been potent. It was every bit as commanding...but had an added lush underpinning that made her think of—well, the exact thing she'd been thinking of since she'd climbed in the Jeep. Or since he'd climbed out of it.

God, maybe she should have gone to the nightclub last night after all. Maybe rubbing bodies with some sweaty, mostly naked beach hunk was what she needed to dull this sudden sharp edge of need.

"Thanks," she said, realizing she'd once again let the silence spin out. He was staring at her, his expression unreadable. When he didn't say anything, just kept looking at her, she rushed on. "If you'll help me get the death machine out of the back, I'll return it, then hop the water taxi over and be back as fast as I can."

The look of disappointment was brief, so brief she'd have missed it entirely had she not been looking at him as intently as he was looking at her. But he was really nice to look at. And not just his hard face and wide, welcoming smile. His body, even in regulation pants and polo shirt, was rugged-looking and fit. Definitely...inspiring.

"Why don't you let me handle the scooter return?" he said easily, covering his disappointment over... what? she wondered.

Had he expected she'd invite him to the resort to wait there while she cleaned up? And why did he want to go? To ogle the surroundings—and the guests? Or to, perhaps, ogle her up close and personal? She shivered a little at the idea and quickly slid out of the Jeep to cover her reaction. One thing she already knew about Sean Gannon—he didn't miss much.

"I'd offer to have you come over to the resort to wait, but they don't allow unregistered guests to—"

He raised his hand and smiled, his expression open and easy now. "No, that's fine. I'm okay here."

Maybe she'd imagined the look of disappointment. He certainly looked as though he didn't care one way or the other. "Okay, then. It's just...I thought..." She shook her head. "Never mind."

His smile flashed wider and he shifted his weight, but didn't move closer. Still, somehow it felt as if he was. "I'll admit that I can't shake this feeling that as soon as I let you out of my sight, you'll vanish. Like a mirage or something I just dreamed up."

The sincerity of his tone made her pause. So...he did care one way or the other. Her skin warmed and her heart tripped just a bit faster. "I'm no mirage. And I won't stand you up." She smiled. "Besides, a Patrick ruling is never vacated."

"I'll remember that." He slid out of the Jeep and dislodged the scooter from the rear before she could search out any deeper meaning in that statement. He rolled the scooter around to her side of the vehicle. "I'll handle this and be waiting right here."

"Wait, you'll need the ticket stub and the—"

"No, I won't. Trust me, you're not only going to have no problem returning this, you're going to get a full refund for the rental price, as well."

"But—"

"Consider it your half of dinner. But you shouldn't have to pay for a broken-down rental."

She didn't bother to argue. Partly because he was absolutely right, although she'd have probably just mentioned the malfunction to the attendant and let it go at that. She listened to arguments all day long in her professional life. She wasn't about to have one on vacation. But mostly she dropped the issue because he had this set to his jaw that told her it wouldn't have done her any good to argue anyway.

"Thank you," she said sincerely, then grinned. "And may I say that when you play Good Samaritan, you're really thorough."

"I believe in always being really thorough," he said. Again, with no overt inflection to any word he'd uttered.

And yet she had to resist squirming in her capris. Probably it was just her overheated imagination. Or the overheated air. Or both. Then he smiled and she thought, *Or not.*

"Me, too," she finally said. It was the best she could manage, because he was still holding her gaze with that direct one of his own.

They both continued to stand there, neither one of them making the first move to walk away.

A bell clanged, announcing that another water taxi had just docked and was taking passengers.

"I should go."

He merely continued to stare.

"The water taxi—" She didn't even try to finish when he propped the scooter against the Jeep and silently stepped closer to her. The rest of her breath left her when he lifted his hand. What would his touch feel like? she wondered as her pulse began to thrum inside her body.

She sucked in a small gasp as he almost brushed her cheek...then slid off her sunglasses instead. She wasn't sure if she was disappointed...or close to climaxing.

"There," he stated quietly. When she raised her eyebrows in question, he smiled. "I had to know."

"What?" she breathed.

"Blue or brown."

She absently realized he was talking about her eye color. It was hard to think straight with him standing so close, almost touching her, and with her dying to know what it would be like to have him touching her, wanting, needing to know, ridiculously so. And all she had to do to find out was to reach up on her tiptoes and— "Did you win?" she said abruptly.

"Win?" he repeated, though he didn't sound as if he really cared what she meant. He was too busy gazing at her, so directly...so intently.

"The b-bet," she stammered, hearing her voice dip down an octave or so. "Blue. Or brown." Her breath was shaky as he shifted another infinitesimal fraction of space closer. "Did you? Win?"

"Yeah," he said, his voice a shade deeper, a shade less flat. "I did."

They were talking, but it was becoming rapidly apparent that the words themselves weren't important as there was another dialogue going on entirely. The kind that didn't rely on speech for communication.

"Good," she said, the word barely more than a breath.

"I have another."

"Bet?"

He merely nodded.

"About?"

"This." He leaned his head down and just like that he pressed those incredible lips against hers. Not demanding, but not at all tentative. Just testing... exploring...finding out...whatever it was he needed to find out.

And it seemed the most natural thing in the world to respond, to lean into the kiss and do some exploring of her own. He tasted fresh, with a little salty tang from the sea air. She felt a moan build in the base of her throat as he opened his mouth and coaxed her to do the same. She had an almost desperate need for him to touch her. Her face, her hair, anywhere. This simple touching of lips was almost excruciating in how it could be so overwhelming...and yet make her feel so deprived at the same time. She wanted more.

He teased his tongue into her mouth and the moan was wrenched from her as she accepted it—almost greedily. She couldn't have rightly given her middle name at the moment, her thoughts had scattered so rapidly the instant his mouth had touched hers. The world had tilted somehow and everything that made sense was suddenly all jumbled up. When she didn't think she could stand the sweet torture one second longer, he finally—mercifully—slid his hands to her shoulders, turned her fully into him, leaning back against the Jeep so he could accept the weight of her body framed so perfectly against his.

She was sinking in the blissful cloud of ecstasy he'd created, completely willing to forget she was standing in a public parking lot, kissing a perfect stranger. Perfect. God knew the kiss alone was as close to perfection as she'd ever come. Come.

Dear Lord, could she ever.

Images of doing just that sprang fully realized into her mind at the same instant he settled her weight between his thighs. The contact was electric...and had the effect of splashing cold water on a hot wire. Sizzle and steam...and the fear of getting burned. She pulled away, gasping in a breath of air as the reality of what they were doing, where they might have taken it— right there in the parking lot, no less—sank in.

She couldn't act horrified, though part of her—the part that had spent an entire lifetime understanding the role proper decorum played in the life of a public figure—wanted to. It had been too incredible, and she'd been too obviously enjoying it, to pretend otherwise. Sean pushed away from the Jeep and reached instinctively for her hips, to steady her as she stumbled a step back from him. As soon as she had her balance, he let her go.

She stemmed the urge to look around the lot, to find out just how big an audience they might have had. It wasn't all that hard. She couldn't seem to tear her gaze away from his.

"I suppose I should apologize for that," he said, his voice now delectably hoarse. "Or at least tell you that I don't make a habit of kissing women I've only just met."

She smiled, suddenly not caring who was watching. Sean Gannon had a way of looking at her that made her feel as if she was the only person in the room...or parking lot, as the case may be. And she decided maybe it was time to let go of a lifetime of proper decorum and do what she'd come here to do...relax. Enjoy life. Leave all her worries behind. "Actually, I'm more interested in finding out if you resolved that other bet you made with yourself."

His smile twitched to a grin and his eyes flashed in that dangerous way. "I did. Except I lost this one."

Surprised, she said, "Oh?"

He reached out, snagged the edge of her hand with his, hooking his finger around her pinky and pulling it up between them. "I bet you couldn't taste as incredible as I imagined you could. And I was wrong."

She looked down at their loosely linked hands,

thinking it was almost a more intimate gesture than his kiss. But she liked the way he had the urge to continue touching her, connecting himself to her in some way. She understood the need, because she felt it herself. "Wrong?" she asked, lifting her gaze back to him and thinking, *God, how long has it been since I so shamelessly flirted with a man?*

Never, was the instantaneous—and honest—answer. But then, she'd never been alone on an exotic island. Alone with a man like Sean Gannon.

He tugged her pinky, just a little, but she shuffled a step closer. "Completely wrong," he said, his smile lazy and the light in his eyes distinctly and unapologetically predatory.

She knew she had a decision to make, and that she had to make it fast. But in her day-to-day life, decisions were weighty matters, only being handed down after intense scrutiny and in-depth analysis of all the presented facts. Now, however, she didn't have that luxury. Sean Gannon wanted her. Right here. Right now. And damn if she didn't want him back. It should be more complicated than that.

But certainly he was a man who understood boundaries, a man who had built a life based on a code of conduct, knew that rules were made for a reason. A man who wouldn't pursue beyond what she was willing to give. Which was, of course, the big question here.

What was she willing to give?

Everything, her body and mind screamed. At least for the next couple of hours. Maybe the next couple of days. Surely she could afford herself that luxury, here of all places. The luxury of letting go, of taking what she wanted. With no regrets. Only intensely wonderful memories of a place out of time, spent with a man far outside of her world.

"Completely wrong?" she repeated.

He dropped her pinky and reached for her hips, pulling her to him in one smooth yank, settling her weight on him, his grip just firm enough to discourage her from stepping away again. Not that she would have. Everything lined up so perfectly, so... She shuddered as she braced her hands on his chest.

"You far surpassed anything I could have dreamed up," he murmured, already lowering his mouth to hers. "Are you a dream, Laurel Patrick? You sure taste like one."

A shiver raced over her when he brushed his lips along hers.

"Maybe dreams aren't such a bad thing to have," she murmured, moving her lips to the sandpapery smooth skin of his jaw. His swift intake of breath when she pressed a kiss just beneath that hard curve was as intoxicating as it was seductive.

"Yeah," he murmured, his voice a hoarse rasp. "Because, occasionally, one of them comes true."

He slid one hand around her neck and moved her mouth back to his. This time the kiss was demanding, consuming. And she didn't even consider holding back. She let her hands slide up his chest and leaned more fully into him. He was rigidly hard...everywhere. It made her feel soft, feminine and eminently desirable. Not a familiar feeling for a woman who spent most of her time in a shapeless black robe, dealing with men who mostly just waited for her to make the slightest hedge in passing judgment, to give them the slightest indication of a weak spot.

Well, Sean Gannon had only been in her company for less than an hour or two...and he'd found just about every weak spot she had. Certainly the sweetest ones anyway.

When he finally lifted his mouth from hers, they stayed where they were, all but mesmerized by one another. For how long, she couldn't have said. But not too many seconds later yet another bell sounded, indicating the last water taxi had not only left, but they'd been tangled up in each other for so long, another one had arrived.

"About this resort," Sean murmured. "Do you really think—"

Laurel smiled, judgment decided upon, ruling made. She would never have another opportunity like this one. Besides, she'd already asked herself the crucial question: would she regret it if she didn't?

And didn't she already have enough regrets in her life?

"I'm thinking that if a judge and a U.S. Marshal can't figure out a way to get you on that island—" she began, but he stopped her.

"Actually, I was going to ask if you'd be willing to skip the shower and change." He looked directly into her eyes in that way he had, and her fingers dug into his chest of their own volition. "Because the clothes don't matter. And we're just going to get sweaty all over again."

Her pulse shot up like a skyrocket. And the muscles between her legs clenched almost painfully in response. "Are we now?" she asked, unsure why she was continuing to provoke him. Except to find out what would happen when she pushed him too far.

He slid his hand up from her neck and slowly

pulled the soft band from her ponytail. Her hair dropped down to her shoulders in a wavy bob, which he pushed away from her face with surprisingly gentle fingers.

"Aren't we?"

She knew what he was asking, just as she knew he already knew the answer. But she liked that he wanted them both to state their intentions. "I believe we are, yes."

He skimmed his fingers along her jaw, then rubbed the tip of one across her lips. "Well then, I think we should ditch this little scooter and go find someplace to have a nice, quiet dinner."

She was already nodding, assuming what he'd been about to say. It took a second or two for his words to register. "What? Dinner?" She'd already been mentally undressing them both and—

Now the wolf smile came out in full. "It's a long night."

Dinner as foreplay. The idea should have made her impatient. She was ready now, dammit. And it should have made her a bit worried. Worried that with too much time, she'd talk herself out of what she'd just finished talking herself into. Only the idea of getting to know him better intrigued her just about as much as the idea of letting him put those hands, and that mouth, on her.

"Yes," she finally responded. "It certainly is." And yet Laurel was pretty damn sure it was all going to go by way too fast. Maybe he had the right idea, after all. Savor each moment. Drag it out. Make it last.

Because when it was over...it was over.

4

WHAT IN THE HELL had he been thinking, asking her to dinner first? The wine hadn't even been served and he was already dying to get her out of there and out of those brand-new vacation clothes...and into his bed.

He'd thought to stop at Sam's, sit on the rear deck, eat broiled snapper as the sun set, and get to know each other better. He needed to understand if this unmanageable desire he suddenly had for her existed simply because she was an appealing and willing woman? Or if it was because of her, specifically...and he was just incredibly lucky that he'd stumbled across her at a time when he had nothing better to do than get to know her better. That made him think about the topic that had been occupying his mind just before he'd almost run her over. His earlier conviction that when he met the right person, he'd just know.

He shook off that thought. He had too much swirling around in his fevered mind as it was. He fiddled with the menu, which wasn't for Sam's. That parking lot had proved to be packed, so he'd driven closer to Morning Star and eventually found a small restaurant tucked below a resort on the opposite side of the cove from his hotel. He could see the lights twinkling from the rooms of his hotel and the glow of the bonfire still roaring on the beach.

"Do you know what you want?" Laurel asked.

He pulled his gaze away from the streaks of gold limning the water in the cove and laid his menu down without looking at it. He looked directly at her instead. "I think I do."

Her grip on the menu tightened and she swallowed. Then she closed her menu, as well. "Me, too."

His lips twitched. "Does it have anything to do with seafood?"

She smiled and he liked the confidence he saw in her eyes. "Not unless you plan on going swimming first as a way to draw out this torture even further."

He slid his hand across the table, let his fingertips drift over the backs of her fingers, liking the slight shiver that raced over her. "Torture? Gee, most women I take out to dinner appreciate the chance to have someone else cook them a meal."

She lifted one shoulder in a light shrug, the setting sun highlighting the teasing glint in her eyes. "I'm not most women."

"On that we're agreed."

She arched an eyebrow, but he merely held her gaze steadily.

"So, is it the company then?" he asked.

"If your company was in question," she continued, "I'd hardly have agreed to dinner. Much less..."

She let that last part trail off, her boldness faltering, then disappearing completely. She went to slide her hand away from his touch, but he covered it, held on.

"Laurel." He waited until she looked at him again. "You know what? Let's have dinner. Maybe a walk on the beach. Talk. I enjoy your company. I'd like to have it for as long as you'll allow. Period."

She opened her mouth, then closed it again on a

short laugh. "Thank you," she said finally. "I guess I'm not as cosmopolitan as I'd wanted to believe."

Now he laughed. "Suave is not exactly my middle name."

"I don't know, you were pretty smooth back there on the dock."

"Then you didn't feel my knees knocking together." *Or my heart trying to pound its way out of my chest.* He sat there, knowing he wanted her more than he wanted his next breath, feeling a bit poleaxed by the intensity of it...and yet he'd settle for dinner, conversation, a short stroll. If it meant keeping her around a bit longer.

Which answered his earlier question. It *was* about her, not opportunity and availability. If he were home, yes, he'd be more than willing to date her, court her, do what was necessary to earn the right to intimacy with her. And he'd probably even enjoy the journey as much as the destination. Despite the nagging physical need, he was truly enjoying himself. Desire just added a nice edge to the whole thing, especially now that he knew she was feeling it herself.

Of course, the downside to this whole scenario was that he wasn't home, which meant he didn't have unlimited time to plan and execute a serious pursuit. In fact, what he had was dinner. And whatever time together she decided to give him afterward. And then...*pfft.*

He didn't even know her yet, and it still pissed him off. Fate had finally put a woman in his path who literally stopped him in his tracks...only to serendipitously do it at a time when he couldn't explore the possibilities with her. Beyond dinner.

Which he was wasting with all this meandering introspection.

"So...snapper?" he asked lightly, or as lightly as he was able. "Or steak?"

She held his gaze for another second, then slid her hand free so she could open the menu again. Sean curled his fingers into his palm and slid his own menu closer, then flipped it open. And he tried like hell not to give in to the urge to shove his chair back, yank her out of hers and carry her out of this place like a goddamn caveman.

Jesus, Gannon.

She looked over the top of her menu. "Snapper."

He meant to glance up, just for a second, then look right back at his menu. He had to get a grip—both physically and mentally—before he made a complete ass out of himself or, worse, made her feel uncomfortable. *Jack the intensity level way down, buddy.* Dinner. Maybe a walk. Talk.

Then *pfft*.

He really had to work at remembering that last part.

He was a man who prized control, had spent years developing it on many professional levels. So why in the hell didn't he seem to have any around her? He glanced up...and was instantly lost. Hooked, totally, on that face, those eyes, that half smile.

"So, did they really?"

"What?" he asked.

"Did they really shake? Because it might have been mine."

What was she talking about?

At his confused look she said, "Your knees."

"Knees," he repeated, too busy staring at her

mouth to really care what in the hell she was talking about.

"You don't really want steak or snapper, do you?" she asked softly, steadily.

He merely shook his head, thinking honesty at this moment was probably stupid but unable, or unwilling, to be anything else with her. He wanted no regrets. Beyond his biggest one, that is. That he hadn't met her anywhere else, at any other time or place, than here and now.

She laid down her menu and stood. She stepped around the corner of the table and held out her hand.

"But—"

"Walk. Talk. I need that much: First."

Her hand was steady, as was her gaze, but he found his own traveling down her body. To her knees. And he smiled then. They were, in fact, quivering. Just a little.

He shoved back his chair, tossed a few dollars on the table to make up for taking up space for the ten minutes they'd been there...then took her hand. Small, fine-boned, but not delicate. At least not fragile. Her slender fingers entwined with his much wider ones, yet he sensed her strength was somehow equal to his, maybe greater. After all, the simple touch made more than his knees quiver. In fact, it sent a little spike of energy...or something, through his entire system.

They stepped outside and the night breeze snatched at their clothing, pulling it then plastering it against them as it whipped gently, warmly, around them. There was a small sign with an arrow pointing to a narrow stone pathway that meandered down to the shore. She tugged his hand.

"You sure you don't want to eat? Just because I—"

"I don't think I could, anyway." She laughed a little. "I have all these butterflies in my stomach." She glanced up at him. "Maybe later?"

Later. That was a word he wanted to hear in conjunction with her as often as possible. "Yeah, definitely." She went to move down the first set of stairs, but he held her back, just for a moment. "Just so you know, there's one or two flapping around inside me at the moment, too."

Her smile softened, relaxed, widened.

It took incredible willpower not to drag them both toward the front of the restaurant, to where his Jeep was parked, and race around the cove to his hotel. Hell, at the moment he felt as though he could just fly there without benefit of transportation. Instead he smiled back, squeezed her hand a little and led her down the stone stairs.

After the first curve in the path, the lighting from the restaurant and hotel situated above it was almost completely extinguished.

"Looks like we missed the show," she said, pointing to the last sliver of orange that was about to slip behind the horizon.

Sean guided her down a steep part of the steps, beyond the small stand of trees, to a longer, straighter part of the path that provided them with an uninhibited view of the sky. He looked up. "I think the next show is just about to begin, though."

They paused, both looking up, waiting for the first star, then the next, to twinkle to life. From somewhere up the hill, music started. He'd seen a small stage in a corner of the restaurant, had wondered briefly if he'd get to dance with her. The music was slow, throbbing, wafting downward, dropping over them like a soft, filmy net, encapsulating them. It seemed the most natural thing in the world to turn her into his body, pull her close and move to the rhythm.

When he wrapped one arm around her waist, she did the same. Their other hands remained linked, swaying loose and relaxed down by their thighs. They were silent, as if neither wanted to break the spell. She eventually let her cheek drift to his shoulder, and he nudged his nose into her hair. She smelled like salt tang and island air and something else that was probably all her. He wanted to know more about that last part, wanted to know her well enough that he could identify her by her scent alone. Somehow he didn't think it would take all that long. One dance, maybe.

They swayed together as stars continued to spark to life overhead.

Sean slid his hand up her back, cupped the nape of her neck, liking the feel of the silky slide of her hair as it caressed his skin. She tipped her head back easily and it seemed the most natural thing in the world to dip his lips to hers, take her mouth and sink into another soul-searing kiss.

And yet her smile made him pause. "What?" he asked, a breath away.

"I was just thinking."

They kept swaying. "Is that a good thing?"

"I don't know. I was thinking that it's amazing what a little music on a starlit path can do to make a girl feel very..."

Sean's lips quirked. "Cosmopolitan?"

Laurel laughed, but nodded.

Sean stared down into her eyes, so open, so expressive. He wondered how she kept them shuttered during a trial, how she could ever maintain the impassive demeanor so important to her position. His grin faded slowly and he smoothed the palm of his hand around so he could stroke her jaw then rub his thumb across her lips.

Her shudder of delight made his body grow hard. Harder. Having her brush, even lightly, against him had been sweet torture.

"We haven't done the talking part yet," he said.

"We will," she said.

He could only nod. At that moment it seemed impossible that this couldn't go on indefinitely, that they didn't have the luxury of time on their side. A whole world of time, a whole world of possibilities. He couldn't seem to make himself understand, much less believe, how limited this was going to have to be. "Yes, we will."

"I feel like..." She stopped, shook her head, smiled that half smile of hers.

He turned her face back to his. "Like we have so much to talk about...but very little needs saying right now?"

She stilled, just for a moment, but he understood.

"Sort of terrifying, isn't it?" he asked softly.

"Completely."

He pulled their joined hands up and turned hers so he could press a kiss to the backs of her fingers. "Laurel—"

She shook her head, pressed her finger to his lips. "Later. We'll have time."

He wanted to ask how she could be so sure, but he nodded instead, wanting to believe. Wishing he had more confidence in fate.

She moved away first, pulling him back up the path.

"No walk, either?" he asked.

She grinned over her shoulder. "I'm not much for getting sand in uncomfortable places."

He laughed. "Oddly enough, I mentioned something about that very sentiment earlier today."

"Something else we agree on, then."

She hit the top of the path and he tugged on her hand, the momentum swinging her around and right into him. "Something else? What was the first thing?"

She lifted up on her toes, took his face in her hands and kissed him. No gentle peck, no teasing come-on. She flat-out kissed him. A heartbeat later, he was kissing her back. Things rapidly escalated from there.

She broke away first, hand to her chest, face flushed, but laughing. "That we'll never make it to the room if we do any more of that here."

"Ah."

"Ah." She danced up the stairs that led around to the front of the restaurant and the parking lot. "Race you to the car."

She was gone before he could answer.

He caught up to her and grabbed her waist an instant before she reached the Jeep. She shrieked as he spun them both around, falling into the passenger seat. She was sprawled across him, both of them breathless with laughter. He pushed her hair back from her face with his fingers. "And here I said I wasn't going to chase beautiful women around the island while I was here."

"I can't imagine why. You're quite good at it."

He grinned. "I was inspired."

"How far away did you say your hotel was?"

"About five minutes."

She crawled off of him, then dragged him out of the seat. "Good. I won't have time to lose my cosmopolitan edge between here and there." She ducked past him and climbed into the passenger seat. "But you better hurry. It might be a Cinderella-type deal."

He stood there, thinking he'd had it right all along. With the right person, you just knew. The hell with *pfft*. Grinning like a fool, he scooted it around the back of the Jeep and hopped in. "Cinderella, huh?"

She folded her hands in her lap, pressed her knees together and gave him a regal look. "One never knows."

Suddenly he had no problem picturing her in charge of an unruly courtroom, although he was beginning to suspect that Judge Patrick's courtrooms were rarely out of order.

"So, you're saying we only get until midnight?"

She maintained the regal pose as she regarded him in the moonlight. "I suppose that depends. Are you claiming to be my Prince Charming?"

"In all honesty, I've never once been called a prince."

Her lips twitched. "Well, honesty will get you places being a prince never would."

His eyes widened. "Really?"

She nodded.

He leaned closer. "Can I honestly tell you, then, just how I plan on keeping the princess locked in my tower beyond the midnight deadline? Making her forget there ever was a deadline?"

She shivered, rubbing her arms, and he knew it wasn't the night air, as the temperature was still quite balmy. "By making me forget I ever came up with this stupid princess idea in the first place?"

He stroked her cheek, her lips, then slipped his hand behind her neck and pulled her mouth up to meet his. "Not a stupid idea," he murmured against her lips. "I'm just glad we already cleared up my princely status, or lack of one, so you won't be in for any surprises later."

"Oh," she said, feigning disappointment. "Not any?"

She took his breath away. Serious one minute, silly the next. Confident one minute, unsure the next. Smart, sharp and fast with a comeback. He'd never— not ever—played with anyone like this. She was like some kind of drug and he was already addicted.

Sure, maybe it was the island air, the freedom of being a thousand miles from home. But he didn't think so. "I guess we'll have to see about that," he responded.

He felt as though he was falling into her as he took her mouth, her tongue, toyed with her, played with her, encouraged her to do the same. When they finally came up for air, she collapsed limply back in her seat. "Suddenly five minutes is seeming like a really long drive."

Sean laughed. And couldn't agree with her more. "Well, if I don't put my hands on the steering wheel, instead of on you, it's going to be a hell of a lot longer."

She pointed toward the main road. "Home, James." Then she rolled her head toward him and, even in the moonlight, the glint in her eyes sparkled. "Please."

"I aim to do exactly that."

She moaned softly, then turned her head to stare at

the road ahead, wrapping her arms around her waist. As if she were so sensitized that even the night air was stirring her up. He suspected it was...because he was feeling exactly the same way. The handful of miles back to the hotel seemed like a cross-country trip. His grip on the steering wheel tightened with every passing minute, just to keep him from touching her.

In fact, when he finally, blessedly, pulled into the hotel parking lot, he wasn't even sure he could trust himself to make it to the room if he so much as brushed against her. He felt like a stupid, undersexed teenager. Until he looked at her. And then he felt very adult, with very adult needs, cravings, desires. He grinned. And, thankfully, as an adult, he knew just how to go about getting them all assuaged.

Fortunately his brain was still functioning well enough to allow him to make a stop in the lobby gift shop.

"You weren't kidding when you said you didn't come here to chase island women," was the only comment she made when he stopped at the small array of contraceptives on the end of one rack.

He looked up at her. "No, I wasn't." And they both knew, had already known, that this was something they didn't normally do. Wouldn't do. Except they could no longer imagine not doing it. As soon as possible, please.

She raised an eyebrow when he grabbed the value-pack box instead of the individual packets. He just smiled and shrugged, then laughed when she reached past him and tossed another box on the counter with his. "Apparently *I'm* the one in for a few surprises," he said. "I just hope I'm up to the challenge."

She looped her arm through his as they strode across the lobby to the elevator. "I didn't say *which* midnight."

His body leaped in response to that, the very words he so wanted to hear. That this didn't have to end so soon. He didn't want to think about endings, though. He was too busy anticipating the beginning.

The elevator doors slid open and fortunately no one got on with them. He had her up against the wall before the doors slid shut. "Do you have any idea what you do to me?"

She was already panting. "Oh, I have a pretty fair clue."

He pushed his hips into hers. "Do you realize I have never, not ever, been this incredibly wired to have someone?"

She moaned softly and pressed her hips right back into his, making his knees buckle just a little. "You're the one who wanted to draw things out."

He barked a little laugh. "Draw things out? Damn, I still don't even really know you."

She reached for his face, stroked it with her palms, tilted his gaze down to hers. "That's the oddest thing of all, isn't it? I don't know you, either. So explain to me why this feels so familiar, so natural? In fact, it feels like one of the rightest things I've ever done." She laughed a little. "God, I hope I don't feel like an idiot for saying that come morning."

He leaned in, kissed her, only gently this time. So at odds with how ravenously hungry he was for her, it shocked him almost as much as it surprised her. "I don't want any regrets," he murmured. Although he already knew he'd have a boatload. Not for making love to her. No, never. He was going to regret not having more time here, where time had no meaning. He wanted time to get past making love...to see if they could fall *into* it.

Talk about foolish.

5

THEY STUMBLED INTO his hotel room, hands all over each other. Laurel helped Sean tug his polo shirt over his head so she could finally get to run her hands all over that incredibly hard chest of his. He captured her lips with his, pinned her roving hands to the wall as he pillaged her mouth with his tongue, taking his sweet time, until she could barely remain upright.

He finally lifted his head, looked at her, eyes glittering. "I want to take my time. I want to make this last for hours, days, weeks. And I want to inhale you, consume you, take you. All of you, right now."

No, she wasn't going to regret a single second of this. "I know."

He slid his hands down her arms, tugged her shirt over her head, then wove his fingers through the tangle her hair had become on the drive back. "I need more hands."

She laughed a little. He'd sounded so serious. "You're doing quite well with the ones you have," she said, her voice thready.

"I want to peel you out of these clothes, but I don't want to let you go. I don't want to stop watching your eyes. Do you know they tell a thousand stories? Do you know I want to hear them all?"

He took her breath away. The things he said to her, every word so honest, so baldly spoken, she wasn't even sure if he was aware of what tumbled from those carved lips of his.

And then he was kissing her again, taking her hands and putting them on his chest, groaning deep in his throat when she began to caress every swell and valley of muscle, the swirls of hair that lightly covered his chest, the rigidly hard nipples that edged beneath her fingertips. He took their kiss even deeper, and then she was the one groaning when his hands slipped up her back and flicked open the hooks of her bra. The very idea of his heated flesh sliding over hers... She shuddered hard when he pulled the straps down her arms, never breaking their kiss.

His thumbs brushed the sides of her breasts, skated in, across her nipples, making her gasp, then moan, as he skimmed his palms down to grip her waist...and rubbed his chest against hers. She hooked shaking fingers into his waistband.

"I'm going to be vertically challenged here momentarily," he murmured against her kiss-swollen lips.

"Marshals like being challenged, don't they?" she said, trailing kisses along the edge of that oh-so-hard jaw of his. How could he be so rock hard, so chiseled, from cheeks to lips to chin to chest...and yet one smile set his eyes to twinkling and everything shifted. He went from trained professional...to rogue bad boy. And she wanted them both. On her. In her. Dear God.

He pulled her away from the wall and back-walked her to the bed. "I'd rather face this challenge horizontally."

"Sissy," she teased.

He lifted his head from where he'd been nibbling an intensely erotic path from her neck to her shoulder.

"Sissy? Is that what you just said?" His eyes gleamed, but it was all sexual taunting.

Oh, could she learn to love teasing this man. "I believe that was the word I used." She managed to lift one shoulder in a nonchalant shrug, which was amazing considering she was about one brush of a tongue away from kneeling at his feet and begging him to do whatever he wanted, however he wanted.

He yanked her up tight against him, wrapping one arm firmly around her back. She gasped. He was so hard. She wanted to absorb the entire surface of his body into hers. Preferably without the rest of these damn clothes impeding the sensations.

"You want to be taken standing up then?"

Her knees wobbled dangerously, as did her heart. "Not if you don't think you're...up to it."

His fierce gaze was matched only by the incredibly wicked grin that little comment earned her. Oh, yes, teasing him was delicious, dangerous fun. Who knew courting danger could be so intoxicating?

"Back up."

Laurel's eyes widened at his tone. The teasing glint was definitely there in his eyes, but his voice was all business. As though he was used to giving orders.

"That wall," he said, lifting his chin. "There."

"You need a wall to prop me on?" she commented recklessly, just barely managing the comeback. Not only were her knees threatening to give way, she was pretty sure if she so much as rubbed her thighs together at that moment, she'd—

"No. But you will."

A little shudder worked its way through her body. She should have known better than to mess with a man who'd had all kinds of special training. "Pretty sure of yourself."

He took her hips and swung them both around so her backside snugged up against the overstuffed arm of the couch. "Yes," he told her, keeping his hands on her, bringing his half-naked, rock-solid body excruciatingly close...but not quite touching any other part of her exquisitely sensitized body. "I am."

He nudged her back until the soft padded arm pushed up against her, then carefully placed her hands on either side, pressing her fingers into the cushion. "Hold on."

She opened her mouth, but finally decided it might be better to shut up at that point. She'd goaded him far enough. Besides, she was dying to know what his plans for her were, so hyper aware of her semi-naked state...and so unconcerned about it. Her level of trust was probably the height of foolishness...and yet she knew his only goal was pleasure.

And she didn't think his confidence was misplaced.

He leaned in and she automatically lifted her hands without thinking, wanting to rub her fingers over his soft, bristle-short hair. But he pressed them back down. "Uh-uh." Then he slowly traced the very tip of his tongue along the line of her jaw to just beneath her ear. The palms of his hands had smoothed up her thighs to rest on her waist. "Next time, we do it my way. And you can be in charge."

"Next time," she breathed, wondering if she'd survive that long. She moaned softly and let her eyes drift shut as he pressed hot, pulse-spiking kisses along her neck and collarbone, then shifted his weight lower as he dropped his mouth, tongue and fingers along the front of her body.

She gasped sharply and arched her back when he teased one nipple between his lips and the other between his fingers.

And when she didn't think she could stand the sweet torture another moment, he moved lower. Who knew her navel was an erogenous zone?

Sean Gannon apparently.

He opened the skinny zipper on her hip with his teeth, then peeled the stretchy fabric down her hips...down her legs...with maddening slowness.

"Oh, ho," Sean said, his accompanying chuckle low and sexy. "Now we know that Judge Patrick likes to wear a little silk beneath her robes."

"I, uh— Oh!" Her panties came off with a quick snap that shocked her into opening her eyes, only to find Sean flicking a small knife back into the all but invisible sheath on the inside of his waistband.

"Dear Lord."

"He can't help you now." He grinned up at her. "You signed a deal with the devil."

Laurel couldn't think of a single retort, except, "Yes."

Sean kissed the tender spot just below her navel. "Don't worry, I'll buy you another pair."

Laurel's hips started moving, she couldn't help it, didn't want to help it. The man's tongue was just everywhere. Except... She shifted, sighed in frustration as he continued toying with her. "If you'd finish what you started, Deputy Marshal, I'll let you cut up anything I own," she said on a pleading groan.

Sean laughed, vibrating the skin of her inner thighs. That alone was enough to make her swear.

"Why, Justice Patrick, such language."

She arched her back, torn between grabbing his

head to push his mouth where she so badly needed it...and slithering to the floor to just let him take his own sweet time.

"Whose idea was it to do this standing up, anyway?" she muttered.

Sean slid his hands up...and his tongue in. A shout of pure rapture escaped her before she could stifle it. Her climax was instant and voracious, a live thing, ripping straight through her, then settling into a pool of hot pleasure that simply quivered endlessly, like ripples in a pond, spreading forever outward.

She barely heard the sound of his trousers hitting the floor, the rustle of the gift shop bag, before his hands were on her hips again. He lifted her so she was sitting on the arm of the couch.

"Wrap your legs—"

She was already one step ahead of him. She grabbed his shoulders, aching for him. He paused, waited for her to look at him. He was magnificent, his face almost rigid with the obvious control he was exerting.

"Are you certain, Laurel?"

Now it was her turn to laugh. "You're joking, right?"

He grinned, only the humor that reached his eyes was almost predatory. "I don't kid around about something like this." His smile faded. "Not with you."

Something melted within her. She had a sneaking feeling it was her heart...or a part of it anyway. "I'm very sure. Thank you for taking care of me." She smiled again. "But don't make me get that sneaky little knife of yours to force you to finish."

His grin was downright wicked. "Well, I think I'm

going to like your turn even better than I've enjoyed mine." He pulled her hips closer and nudged just inside her, making her gasp. "Which is really saying something." Then he drove completely into her, startling a little squeal from her, but only for a moment.

She was already crossing her ankles behind his thighs even as he tugged her tighter into his embrace.

There were no words then, no smiles, no laughter, merely a primal mating the likes of which she'd only read about...and never dreamed could be real.

Sean literally growled through his climax and Laurel couldn't be certain, but she might have growled a bit herself.

Afterward, Sean held her close, his face pressed into her hair. She clung to him, panting heavily, unable to form anything resembling speech. Then his stomach rumbled and they both laughed.

"*Now* he's hungry," she teased.

Sean lifted his head, pushed her hair from her face. "Shower with me, then I'll take you anywhere on the island you want to go."

Laurel smiled into his handsome face, wondering how he could become so dear to her in a matter of hours. It was as if he was meant to be hers, always had been—it had merely been a matter of finding him. She should have been terrified. Somehow, she wasn't. She felt...settled.

She stroked his temple, his cheek, his lips. "Does this hotel have room service?" She rubbed her hands over his now damp brush cut. "I'm feeling a bit selfish at the moment and I don't want to share you."

Something almost fierce sparked in his eyes, making her twitch hard with an instinctive response, but his smile was soft, sexy. "Funny, I was thinking the exact same thing."

SEAN WAS FAIRLY CERTAIN he'd died and gone to a heaven he could have never imagined. Laurel, wild and willing in his arms, wrapped around him, was surely a dream come true. Having her now, standing in a steaming shower, her soft curves wrapped around his as they let the hot water pound down on them, went beyond dreams into some fantasy world he was certain he'd wake up from at any moment. She felt so soft, so perfectly fitted to him, so...right.

He pressed his lips to her hair, felt her fingertips press more firmly into his back as she held him even tighter. They'd teased and laughed as they'd soaped each other's bodies, washed each other's hair. All that slippery fun had only served to rile them both up again, and he'd started kissing her, sliding his hands over her, fingers inside her, teasing her, tormenting her, until she'd come apart for him all over again.

She'd trembled for him, gasped his name as she'd climaxed. And Sean had felt this undeniable humbling, as if some part of him knew the magnitude of the gift she'd blessed him with. And his kisses had gentled, deepened, taken them to some new place, a place with no words, where none were needed. He simply held her now, felt her heart beat against his, as the water beat down on him.

And he felt both incredibly at peace...and more scared than he could ever remember. He wanted Laurel Patrick. Not for one night, not even for one wild week. He *wanted* her. In some deep-down, indefinable way. In a way he would happily spend his life trying to figure out. A part of him knew, had to believe, it was the sex. Along with all those emotions Brett's wedding had riled up in him. Because it was insane to think, to even assume for one second, that she was the one for him. A woman he knew intimately, yet hardly at all otherwise.

Except he knew now, without a single shred of doubt, he could already find her in the deepest dark with nothing to guide him but his instincts.

They'd stood there, in easy silence, comfortable in each other's arms, for so long their skin would be pruning momentarily. And yet he wasn't willing to leave this steam-filled cocoon. The real world lay beyond this room, this hotel, and he selfishly didn't want them to go back out into it. If he could just stay here forever, he would be eternally grateful. Because then she would be his.

His stomach chose that moment to emit another unceremonious growl. She snickered. And just like that, real life was there between them, anyway. When she smiled up at him, so easily, so naturally, it suddenly didn't seem like such a scary place.

He leaned down and kissed her smile, drinking it in, and knew right then he'd do what he had to, to make sure their time didn't end here.

ROOM SERVICE ARRIVED forty-five minutes later, but the time waiting wasn't wasted. They sat on the balcony, each of them sipping a cold bottle of beer, watching the stars twinkle over the bay. He'd told her about his family, his brother's wedding, Brett's work with rescue animals and the earthquake that had led Brett to meet Haley, his bride. He'd told her about his sister Carly's baby girl and how ridiculously besotted his whole family was with her.

"Yourself included?" Laurel had asked.

He'd nodded. "Something about the tiny perfection of all those fingers and toes. It's humbling, you know?" Then he'd laughed. "She captivates me, and totally terrifies me."

Laurel had nodded in apparent understanding. He'd asked about her family then, and she'd just begun to talk about her judicial heritage when the knock on the door had come.

He waved her still when she started to rise. She was wearing a hotel bathrobe and nothing else. "I'll get it." He'd pulled on a pair of running shorts after their shower. "Would you like to eat out here?" There was a steady breeze off the water, but it was warm, as was the night air.

She nodded and tucked her bare toes back through the balcony railing. "That would be great."

"I'll be right back." Barefoot himself, he went to the door, glad she was staying for dinner. He fully intended to convince her to stay for dessert, too... though they hadn't ordered any off the menu. And if he was inordinately lucky, she'd stay the night. Then there would be breakfast together before he was forced to go meet Trenton. That gave him almost nine hours to convince her to spend tomorrow evening with him, too. And every evening after that. During which he'd convince her to continue to see him back in the States.

Because surely between now and then he would tell her he'd decided to take the training job in Alexandria.

It was time to go back home. Any doubts that might have lingered were gone. His parents weren't getting any younger. He missed his siblings—seeing Carly begin her family, giving Clay a hard time, watching Izzy work herself half to death. Maybe he could make her realize that work was only a part of life. The thought of him being the deliverer of that particular advice and Izzy's probable reaction to it almost made him laugh out loud, but the room service waiter was staring at him expectantly. So he tipped him, then commandeered the rolling cart, assuring the waiter he could take care of the delivery from here.

He paused to look at Laurel sitting out on the deck, wet hair combed back from her smooth, clear-eyed face. She was sipping her beer, looking up at the night sky. And something inside his chest settled into place. It was insane. Truly. He might get to know her and realize they had nothing in common other than the exceptional ability to have mind-altering sex with one another. But he didn't think so. She made him laugh, she made him think on his feet, she made him... happy.

So, yeah, he'd tell her about the job. Eventually. Telling her he was ready to settle down—in a town where she happened to work—well, that might be a bit too much for her to deal with so soon. But if that wasn't some kind of sign, he didn't know what was. As though all his stars were lining up just right for him to make this change. Still, he didn't want to risk making her uneasy. Hopefully sometime during their week together he'd know it was the right time, know she'd be as excited by the serendipitous turn their fates were taking as he was. But not tonight.

Tonight, tomorrow, and for a few more tomorrows...this was the time for falling in love. The rest would follow.

LAUREL STRETCHED languorously in Sean's bed. Alone, but deliriously happy. What a decadent wench she felt like. Spending the night with him had probably not been the smartest move for a woman bent on not making any personal commitments in her life for a while. But it would have taken a whole lot more fortitude than she'd had last night, or early this morning for that matter, to walk away from him.

She stared at the ceiling and hugged herself as she played back their night together in her mind. She shivered with remembered pleasure. Dear God, the pleasure. She felt as though she'd immersed herself in sensation after sensation. And in Sean. He was...well, he was perfect. For her. Could being with someone be this simple? She honestly didn't think so. Alan was proof of that. It had to be the island, the escape from real life, from any real responsibilities or stress.

She grinned. Of course that hadn't stopped her from agreeing to see Sean again tonight. Much less staying in his bed and snoozing half the morning away after he'd dressed and gone to work. But multiple orgasms, as she was learning, weakened a woman's ability to say no.

She wasn't really complaining.

She sat up and spied the small gift-store bag lying at the foot of the bed. She dumped it out...and laughed at the pile of tropical-print silk bikini underwear. Then she read the note that had been tucked in with them. "Don't plan on having any of these left by the time you fly back to the States. Yours, Sean."

She grinned, she blushed...she got aroused all over again.

She dragged the covers back and climbed out of bed. What a wanton she'd become, she thought as she padded naked to the bathroom and flipped on the shower. She stretched as steam filled the room. But it felt so damn good, she thought. She'd needed this. The trip away, the wild sex, the fast flirtation, the laughter...the falling a little bit in love.

She froze as that last part tripped through her brain, then laughed. But it sounded phony even to her own ears. Falling in love. Well, okay, falling in lust, that much she'd admit to. But she probably could fall for Sean. They'd talked long into the night last night. He'd told her about his family, about his work for the Marshals Service. He'd sounded so dedicated, it was obvious it was his whole life. She could identify with that.

She grinned, remembering when he'd told her about being part of the Special Operations team, remembering his expression when she'd laughed, telling him she'd already suspected he'd had a bit more than the average training. He'd enjoyed that. She'd told him she'd enjoy having him show her just what other special skills he had.

She'd finished telling him about her judicial ancestry, her father and how proud she was to be part of the Patrick tradition. She didn't talk about her mom, or her unrest with her job and her childhood dreams of being a mother and wife that were still nudging at her. She didn't tell him about Alan and how unsettling his attentions had become. With any luck, that would all be over anyway by the time she got home. Besides, it wasn't the right time for those kinds of confessions, so early in a relation—

She stopped halfway through soaping her hair. Okay, she thought, so maybe you're falling into a bit more than lust. The fact was he lived in Denver. She was in Louisiana. Yes, he was from there—a wonderful bonus. He had family there. But she wasn't going to be able to sustain a long-distance relationship on the occasional holiday visit. She sighed, realizing just how ridiculous she'd sound if she were mulling this over with a friend. For God's sake, she'd just met the man twenty-four hours ago and she was already planning some kind of long-term thing.

And yet she couldn't stop thinking about Sean's quick smile, his laugh, the intense way he looked at her when he spoke...the things he said to her between the soft gasps they made as they pleasured each other. And she knew it wasn't silly to dream of what could be. It was wonderful.

Maybe this was a sign, she thought as she got out and dried herself off. Meeting him here, yet sharing similar roots. She smiled as she slid a pair of the tropical-print panties up her legs, then straightened the impossibly thin little straps over her hips. Was meeting him, wanting him, being tantalized by the possibilities, a sign that she was ready for her life to move in a new direction?

Whoa. "You're taking this way too far." It was an island fling with a man who simply needed a break as badly as she did. Nothing more.

She didn't want to hear that truth, even in her own head. Right now, right here, in Sean Gannon's hotel bathroom, she wanted to dream, she wanted to explore what might be, instead of accept what had to be.

She shifted then, looked at herself in the mirror...and burst out laughing. The steam on the mirror revealed a large heart that Sean must have drawn when he'd showered before leaving for work. In the middle of the heart it read, "C U 2 Nite."

She sighed, feeling more confused than ever. What if this wasn't too much too soon? What if this was just two people helplessly attracted to one another? Island fling be damned. She'd take the week, see where it went. See what kinds of talks they had with one another. See what kinds of decisions they'd want to make when it was time to leave.

Right now was the time for having fun, the time for letting go, for not thinking about anything but the moment.

And maybe falling a little bit in love.

She managed to sustain that fantasy all the way back to the ferry dock. She was humming to herself as she got out of the island taxi and paid the driver. Already thinking about how she was going to while the day away before Sean met her here at the dock at five-thirty. Maybe she'd try snorkeling. There was a bounce in her step as she walked toward the dock. She could see the water taxi just coming in. Perfect timing.

She paused, then stumbled to a complete stop as a man waiting for the taxi turned and spied her. *No. No, it couldn't be. This wasn't happening.*

"Laurel!" he called, a smile splitting across his too perfect face. "Can you believe I'm here? After I got your note, I knew I had to. I cleared my schedule so we could spend some time alone together, work things out."

Alan Bentley walked up to her and hugged her as she stood there, frozen in place.

6

SEAN PULLED onto the main road and headed toward downtown Alexandria. A lot had happened in four weeks. He'd made a lot of decisions, and because of those decisions, his whole life had changed. For the better, he thought, remembering how thrilled his parents had been at the news, how much he was enjoying the challenge of being one of the handful of trainers for the Special Operations program run by the U.S. Marshals at Camp Beauregard. But as he headed toward his new quarters, a small two-bedroom home on the outskirts of Alexandria, his thoughts weren't on any of the changes he had made but on the one change he'd had no control over. Laurel Patrick walking out of his life without looking back.

Was she at the courthouse right now hearing a case? He'd seen her name in the newspapers, in the multitude of columns discussing the big Rochambeau trial she was to preside over, slated to begin in less than a month if there were no further delays. District Attorney Alan Bentley was going after a prominent member of the crime family, Jack Rochambeau, and the whole parish was talking about it. About Bentley's run for public office in next year's election and using this very public trial as his springboard into politics. About the controversial way he'd zoomed up the ladder in the past five years, with many a whispered comment—and some more baldly spoken—that he'd had this judge or that judge somehow pave the way for him.

About the new rumors of a brief involvement with Judge Laurel Patrick nine months earlier, and whether she was the judge whose help would carry him all the way to the state senate. She'd refused to comment on the case, or her personal life. Grainy photos had surfaced, causing a new uproar, but Judge Patrick had continued to refuse to make public comment, other than stating that she wouldn't recuse herself from the case and that her judgment was not in question. Naturally the media was making a circus out of the whole thing. The more Laurel refused to discuss it, the more everyone else did.

Sean just wished they would stop talking about it around him. He'd told no one about his brief involvement with the young justice and didn't intend to. He wanted to forget her. Had spent four weeks trying.

He could sooner forget his middle name. He wanted to be angry with her...and he had been, at first. Then he'd moved here and seen the front-page stories and heard the back-page whispers. Was Alan Bentley the reason Laurel had checked herself out of her hotel hours after she'd left his bed that morning? Was he the "personal crisis" that she had mentioned in the hurried note she'd left at his hotel on her way to the airport? Or was it her father, the state supreme court justice, once a beloved judge in this very parish? Seamus Patrick's tenure on the bench was almost up and there was talk that he'd be casting his hat into the political ring, maybe against the very man currently trying his case in front of Patrick's daughter.

Sean wished he could laugh at the soap opera being played out in the papers and on the news, as so many had before and would no doubt continue to be in the future. Louisiana was nothing if not colorful, both with its characters and its politics. He wished he could remain detached, shrug off the niggling concerns that made the back of his neck itch. His gut instinct told him that something more was going on here...something dark and murky just below the surface—another Louisiana specialty—and that Laurel was likely right smack in the middle of it.

What would she say, he wondered, if he wandered into the courthouse and knocked on the door to her chambers? Would she be surprised in a good way? Or would it upset her that her island lover was waltzing back into her life when it was obviously on the verge of scandal? Would she even agree to see him at all?

He slowed as he reached the turnoff that would take him right by the courthouse. "Move on, Gannon. Get over her," he muttered, not for the first time. But somehow, this time, his car made the turn. And the next thing he knew he was standing outside the door of her chambers, talking to one of the clerks.

"I'm sorry, she's hearing motions at the moment. Is this in regard to one of her cases?" The young man noted the U.S. Marshals insignia on Sean's shirt.

It was sort of a tricky question, Sean thought. It was a case, an upcoming one in particular, that had led him to this spot. "In a way. I do need to speak with her." He'd decided this was the only way he was going to be able to move on, to put their explosive time-out-of-time experience in St. Thomas behind him. And just thinking about it that way made him cringe inwardly. An island romance where the woman left the man high and dry...and the guy couldn't stop panting over what was never going to be. How pathetic and clichéd could he be?

"And your name, sir?" the clerk asked.

It had been a mistake coming here. Of course, his last name was on the name tag on his shirt, so it was likely Laurel was going to hear about his visit anyway. But if he turned around right now, walked out of the building, the—

"Sean?"

His head whipped around so fast he was surprised he didn't get whiplash. How many times in the past four weeks had he heard that voice in his dreams? He'd lost count. "Laurel." She looked the same...and yet completely different. Same face, same expressive eyes, but there was a haunted look about her. No, hunted. Was it because of him?

His instincts said no, that she'd carried that look before she'd seen him in the hallway. Probably borne of the intense media scrutiny of the past few weeks.

"What are you doing here?" Her tone was more surprised than terse, but there was no real hint of welcome in it.

There must have been a million different things he had wanted to say to her, ask her, demand of her. Not a single one came to mind at the moment. He was too busy drinking her in, like a man too long in the desert without water, staring at a sparkling fountain.

They both seemed to notice the more-than-minimally interested clerk at the same time. "Why don't we take this in chambers?" she said quietly, making it sound as if he were there on official business, when she had to know damn well it was anything but.

He merely nodded and followed her inside. Her judicial chamber was small, but tastefully appointed. She immediately walked behind her stately mahogany desk. As if she needed to put a physical barrier between them. Well, she could toss up a brick wall for all he was concerned. Now that he'd come to her, he wasn't leaving without some answers.

Only he couldn't seem to remember the questions.

"Why are you here, Sean?" she repeated quietly. It was then he noted the subtle hint of desperation edging her expression, if not her words.

"I didn't come to make trouble, if that's what you're worried about," he said, irritated without quite knowing why. "Seems like you found enough of that all by yourself."

There was quick flash of surprise, maybe a little hurt, then her expression was once again smooth, removed. "Sometimes it comes with the job," she said coolly.

How had he ever doubted she could be impassive? His irritation flashed brighter. Dammit, she could remove herself emotionally from the rest of the world, but not from him. Not after what they'd shared.

That ridiculously sappy thought should have sent him striding out of the office right then and there. But he'd been one of the two people in that hotel room back in St. Thomas. And sentiment be damned, they had shared something out of the ordinary. And because they had, he didn't hammer her with questions. He simply told her the truth. "I'm here because I've missed you."

Her expression faltered and emotion—the passion he remembered so vividly—flickered briefly to life in her eyes. It was shuttered far too quickly. "I—I'm sorry. About the way things ended."

He wanted to grab her, shake her, kiss the living daylights out of her, force her to admit to—to deal with—the electricity bouncing between them even now. He forcibly relaxed his hands, his posture. "Whatever it was that sent you running...you didn't have to run alone, Laurel."

"I didn't run. I had to return home."

"Because of this trial?"

"My work is like that sometimes. I'm sure you, of all people, understand."

He wanted to shout at her, to demand to know how she could stand there, mere feet away, and not want to feel his hands on her, his mouth on her. Because God knew it was killing him not to touch her. "I do understand. In fact, I made some decisions specifically because my job didn't allow much of a stable lifestyle." He wasn't sure if he wanted to laugh or cry at the alarmed look that flickered across her lovely features. "Don't worry. I made these decisions before I met you. Although I won't lie and say I wasn't less unsure of them once I had. If you'd stayed, I would have explained."

"Explain now. What decisions?"

"I didn't come all the way from Denver to play the lonely puppy begging for attention. I live here now."

Her eyes popped wide and, in that instant, he was absolutely certain he'd been right earlier. Hunted was exactly the emotion he'd seen in her eyes. Along with a healthy dose of fear. Of him? That was ridiculous. But it hurt a great deal more than he was willing to admit. "I'm not stalking you, Laurel. I was offered a permanent training position out at Beauregard. I'd been considering it for some time, and after coming home for my younger brother's wedding, I'd pretty much made up my mind to say yes. Then I met you and it seemed like fate was sending me a neon sign. But it's not my intention to make you uncomfortable. I had hoped—" He broke off, suddenly wishing he'd never done this. It was obvious she wasn't happy to see him, that he'd completely misread everything that had happened in St. Thomas.

Idiot. Brett's getting married and Carly becoming a mother had obviously affected him to a far greater degree than he'd realized. He shook his head. "Never mind. It's not important now." He turned, walked to the door. With one hand on the knob, he turned back, needing—no matter how pathetic—one last look at her. "I just wanted you to know that I would have been there for you, Laurel," he said quietly. "What we had, despite the brevity, affected me on some level that..." God, could he not just leave this woman's life without making a complete and total fool of himself? Apparently not, because he finished by saying, "If you ever need someone you can trust, no matter the reason, call me."

He supposed he'd hoped, in some corner of his mind, that she'd stop him from leaving. Rush out into the hall, tell him she'd made a stupid mistake, that she'd been afraid. Well, that last part at least was true, he thought as he climbed angrily into his car and slammed the door. She was afraid, and if he wasn't so upset with himself for that stupid schoolboy show he'd just put on, he'd have wondered at the real source of it. Because he was right about that hunted look. And that it had likely been there since she'd returned to Louisiana. Long before he'd stepped back into her life. The question was, once he cooled off, what—if anything—was he going to do about it?

LAUREL STOOD THERE, hands braced on the back of her chair, staring at the door of her chambers for long, long minutes after Sean had closed it behind him. Part of her was still stunned—by his sudden appearance, by his shocking announcement that he was now in Louisiana on a permanent basis. He'd known, he said, about the job offer, even before he'd met her. Before they'd sat on his hotel balcony, talking about family and work. And he hadn't told her.

"Well, of course he didn't," she muttered. He'd only just met her, didn't trust her enough to discuss that, and was probably worried that telling her would make her feel unduly pressured in some way. But he would have told her at some point. She knew that now. If she'd stayed. Of course, there was no way of knowing what all he would have shared, but she knew without doubt that Sean Gannon was an honest man. A man with integrity, a man who honored his word, who expected respect and handed it out easily when it was deserved.

Did she deserve it? He'd been angry with her, that much was clear. And she couldn't say she blamed him. It shouldn't have, but the fact that he'd tracked her down, just to tell her he missed her, made her feel better than she had in weeks. Yet it also shamed her. But what else could she have done?

She'd had no choice but to leave, and she'd certainly had no right to drag him into the mess in which she'd found herself smack in the middle. She wished she could have told him how many times she'd wanted to pick up the phone, track him down in Denver, just so she could hear his voice. So she could tell him everything, convinced that somehow, some way, he'd make it all okay. Or at least more bearable. But she couldn't call him then and she couldn't tell him now. Any of it. Because she did know him well enough to know that he'd jump right into the center of it with her, and he didn't understand what was at stake. Because he was an honorable man, he'd expect her to do the right thing, expect her father to do the right thing.

She tugged her chair out and slumped into it, feeling so tired her bones ached. Guilt racked her, even as she seethed in anger at what Alan was doing to her, and to her father, as well—though he was mercifully unaware of it. Of course, her father's role in this also had her upset, angry and confused. But she couldn't confront him. Or wouldn't. He was this close to finishing his term and to retiring, with a golden career record and a potentially bright future in politics. And she knew he was planning to run for office.

Against the very man who was presently blackmailing her.

"Jesus, maybe I should have just crawled back to Alan when he begged me to the first time. Solved everyone's problem." She shuddered at the very idea. Giving in momentarily to her bone-deep fatigue, she folded her arms on her desk and rested her forehead on them. For the umpteenth time, she told herself there had to be an explanation for what Alan had accused her father of doing. But she'd dug into the case Alan had referred to, and she had to admit it looked very fishy. It hadn't even been a splashy case, just a small criminal charge that had ultimately been dropped. But not before a few legal maneuvers had been run and a few motions filed—all in front of her father when he'd held the bench she currently occupied. And all centering on the same man now going to trial in front of her for much larger-scale crimes. Jack Rochambeau.

This was a case Alan Bentley had been thrilled to have the opportunity to prosecute. The obvious reason being that it would help him make an even bigger name for himself before he tossed his hat into the political ring. No one knew of the desperation behind his apparent glee. No one knew that Alan was in a deeply troubling situation, one that had ramifications far bigger than his future in the D.A.'s office.

No one but Alan. And, now, the judge presiding over the trial.

He'd accepted, albeit unknowingly at the time, a

campaign finance deal from the very "family" the district attorney's office was now trying to publicly expose. Which was the real reason he'd fought for the case. So he could lose it. In exchange for a path straight to the state senate door, paved with unlimited laundered funds provided by many of the Rochambeau business connections, Jack Rochambeau was going to receive a Get Out of Jail Free card.

And if Alan failed, more than his future in politics was likely at stake.

But Alan hadn't made it this far without learning how to connive his way out of a bind. He was going to lose this case—he didn't see that he had any choice. The Rochambeaus had him by the short hairs. And, frankly, if Seamus Patrick tossed his hat in the ring for the senate as expected, Alan had likely realized he was going to need the "family's" help if he had a prayer in hell of winning. So Jack was going to get off, and he expected Laurel to help him make that happen, help him unravel what looked to be an airtight case against the arrogant local "businessman." But she was going to help him lose it in such a way that it appeared the D.A.'s office had done everything it could. A technicality here, a difficult ruling by the judge on this motion or that...and Alan's hands were tied. It wouldn't be the significant win Alan had wanted, but he wouldn't be burned too badly for losing it. He'd make sure Laurel took the fall for that.

And if she didn't comply?

Well, she hadn't fallen for his attempts at seduction. Nor had being publicly humiliated caused her to consider stepping down from the case—so she could be replaced by a judge Alan already had in his pocket. So his latest threat was to make sure certain facts about that long-ago case Seamus had overseen would be fed to the media sharks. What a feeding frenzy that would be! Alan hadn't shared the apparent proof with her, but she had enough reason to believe it existed—and it was tearing her apart.

When he'd come to St. Thomas and she'd made it clear, once and for all, that renewing any kind of personal relationship was never going to happen, he'd initially only threatened to destroy her career. If that had been his leverage in getting her to comply with his scheme then, without blinking an eye, she'd have gunned right back and exposed Alan for the lying, manipulating bastard he was.

She'd have taken the fallout that would have surfaced when he countered with supposedly lurid details about their previous relationship. Not that there had been anything remotely lurid about the weekend they'd spent with each other...but Alan would have gone out of his way to make it appear that way. And just as surely, by the time she could prove otherwise, if she could do such a thing, it would have been too late. Her reputation would have been in question, the illustrious Patrick image tarnished, her career irrevocably impaired.

But that wouldn't have stopped her. And Alan had known that, which was why he'd had his ace in the hole. That one shaky case, years before. But with the current media focus on this much higher-profile case involving the same man, the journalists would feast on this new detail and her father's future in politics would be put in serious jeopardy. She had no idea what proof Alan had, or where he'd come by it, but she couldn't risk exposing Alan's scheme, either publicly or to the police. The potential damage to her father was too debilitating.

Her phone rang, making her flinch as she jerked upright, snatching it up before it could ring again. "Patrick."

"I need to see you. Privately."

She stiffened, her stomach revolted. "Absolutely not."

"Oh, I think you will. We need to find a channel of communication. A private channel. Time is ticking away. Plans must be made."

"Al—"

"No names. And don't try to be clever. Just do as I say. Everyone comes out smelling like a rose."

Laurel thought about all the people Jack Rochambeau had hurt—financially, physically, emotionally—during his tenure as the head of one of the most notorious crime families in the state. She thought about the rock-solid case the D.A. had supposedly built against him. Bile rose in her throat. "Where?" she choked.

"That's better. Tonight, eight, our place."

Our place. Laurel could only assume he meant the backwater bridge, where they'd walked and talked after returning from their weekend in New Orleans. Where he'd tried to get her to change her mind about continuing what they'd started. Where she'd seen past the intellect and good looks to the thing that had niggled at her often enough over the course of the weekend to have her ending things before they'd really begun. She'd spied more fully that opportunistic undercurrent that ran just below the river of charm he used to sweep most people off their feet. Laurel, as it turned out, wasn't most people.

Nor had she been interested in being courted for the powerful position she held rather than the woman she was.

"It could have been so different," he murmured into the long silence. "You shouldn't have left me."

Laurel physically recoiled from the image he painted...the underlying threat in his tone. It hadn't taken her very long to discover Alan's controlling, manipulative tendencies. He hadn't wanted to take no for an answer. After all, he'd seen their future together from the moment they'd met. Why hadn't she? Only it wasn't *their* future putting that gleam in his eyes...just his. And he'd expected to use her power, her place in the legal community, her prestige, to get him where he wanted to be.

Sure, she could have kids if she wanted, but there would be no stepping down from the bench. Oh, no, not when he had so many plans. He would give her children, certainly. Kids looked good on campaign posters. They'd make enough money to hire nannies. They would be the ultimate power couple. Alan's aspirations knew no bounds.

Listening to him had made her blood run cold. She'd told him then, with no further attempt to soften the blow, that there was no future between them and never would be. Then she'd literally turned and walked away, leaving him standing there.

Alan hadn't taken it well. Nine months had passed since then. She'd assumed he'd gotten over it, gotten over her, moved on, perhaps already found someone more easily patronized, someone who shared his golden vision of the future.

She'd been wrong. Very wrong.

"Be there. Tonight," he commanded, his voice a soft purr that made the hair on her arms stand on end.

"Fine," she said, her voice a hoarse rasp.

There was a smug chuckle. "Good girl. Or should I say, good Daddy's girl?" The line disconnected before she could utter a response.

Very carefully, with shaking hands, she replaced the receiver, staring at it as if it was some kind of snake that might suddenly leap up to bite her.

"What the hell was that all about?" came a quiet voice from the doorway.

Laurel gasped, hand flying to her chest as she jerked her gaze to the doorway. Sean Gannon stood just inside, his hand still on the doorknob. How much had he heard? She hadn't said anything incriminating. Her mind racing, she tried to corral her thoughts and her fear.

"What—" She had to clear her throat. She sat up straighter, doing her utmost to pull herself together. It was almost impossible. Not when what she wanted to do was to shove her chair back and race into those strong arms that had once been so open for her. Before she'd walked away from them. "What are you doing back here?"

Sean quietly closed the door behind him, then walked toward her desk. His expression was deadly serious. For the first time, she truly appreciated who he was...what he was. "I was in my car, ready to go, but I couldn't shake that look I'd seen in your eyes." He braced his hands on her desk. "That hunted look." He leaned down. "Like the one I see right now."

She wasn't a good enough actress to not blanch at his comment. She'd been yanked too hard emotionally over the past several days to maintain any semblance of normalcy. Especially in front of Sean, who seemed to see so much deeper inside her than anyone ever had.

"So I'm going to ask you again. What in the hell is going on? And you might as well tell me. Because one thing you're going to learn about me is that I don't run."

"I didn't run." She forced the words out. "I chose to leave. It was for the best. Just like leaving now will be for the best." She looked up at him. "Please. It's better if you go. Trust me on this."

"Funny, I was hoping you'd give me that honor." He pushed away from the desk but didn't walk to the door. Instead he pulled up one of the pair of leather padded chairs facing her desk and took a seat.

She looked at him and didn't know which she feared most—that he'd refuse to leave...or that he'd walk out when she needed him most.

7

SEAN STARED AT LAUREL and asked himself who in the hell he thought he was to come barging back in here like the light brigade or something. Whatever her problems were, she'd made it clear they didn't involve him. And that she didn't want them to involve him.

It was that latter thought, underscored by the white-faced fear he'd witnessed when he'd stepped back into the room, that kept him where he sat. "What has you so afraid?" he asked. "And don't tell me you're not. I didn't hear the conversation, but I saw your face. Who's after you?"

It was a guess, but the look of panic that flashed across her face told him he'd gotten it in one.

"It really doesn't concern—"

"I know. And I know you want me out of here in some misguided attempt to protect me. Except if this isn't about me, then I don't know why you'd be worried about that. You know, I do have some background in taking care of myself." He looked her in the eye. "You can trust me on that."

She opened her mouth, as if to argue her point further, then shut it again and slumped back in her seat. "I don't want to fight with you."

"I didn't come here to fight, either."

She looked at him then. "Why did you come back?"

"To help you." He lifted a hand to stop her reply. "Not to interfere. Even if it's just to give you an unbiased ear, a shoulder."

She gave him a look.

He felt a tug at the corners of his mouth. "Okay, so maybe I want to be a bit more involved than that. Sue me. I'm worried about you."

He looked at her then, past the weariness, past the armor she'd probably learned to throw on somewhere back in law school. Sitting on the bench could only have strengthened that instinctive reaction. But behind all of that, he knew there was a woman with a heart, a woman with passion. And that passion had to extend beyond the physical attraction they'd shared. He couldn't say if she had that passion about her work. They'd talked about it, but he hadn't sensed the same fervor in her for her vocation as he had for his. Which begged the question...what did she care enough about to be this afraid of losing?

One thing came to mind. Her father. When she'd spoken of him, of her family legacy, she'd been passionate, she'd been proud.

"I appreciate that," she said quietly. "But I don't need you to worry."

He changed tactics. She *did* need someone to care—it was clear no one else was stepping up for the duty. And here he was, ready and willing to take on the job. "Laurel, tell me one thing. And be honest. If you weren't caught up in the middle of...whatever it is that's eating you up like this...would you be so quick to run me out the door?" He leaned forward, fingers digging into his thighs. "If it makes it easier, I'll be honest first. I've never chased after anyone, and I don't want you to think I'm dogging you because we...because of what we—" He broke off, shook his head, swore under his breath.

"Because we had mind-blowing sex for one night in the islands?" she said, and for the first time he saw a hint of that smile, a hint of that attitude that had so attracted him.

He felt the color rise in his cheeks, but his grin was easy...and made him feel more relieved than he'd thought possible. "Well, since we're being honest, I can't lie and say that didn't have some impact on my feelings about you." His grin faded and her expression sobered, as well. "What I was trying to say was that this isn't something I make a habit of doing. In fact, it's something I never do. I don't have the time or the inclination to chase women down." His lips twitched. "No matter how hot the sex."

She gave him that look, a little eye roll. And he finally started to settle down. This was what he'd come looking to find. That rapport they shared, both spoken and unspoken. So easily, so naturally.

"I came here," he told her, "because I couldn't stop thinking about you. I meant what I said earlier. I missed you. Really missed you. And, yes, I know we haven't known each other all that long, but that didn't seem to matter to us then. That didn't change for me, even after I came back home. There are things I want to share with you, things I find myself wanting to say to you, just to get your reaction. We'd only just begun and, as hard as I tried to forget about it, let it go...I just couldn't." He looked at her, expression as open as he knew how to make it, heart right out there on his sleeve where it had never once been before. "So I'm asking you, when you left, was it easy to forget? Was I easy to forget?"

She shook her head. "No," she said softly.

"Would you have walked away if not for this crisis?"

She looked at him for so long, he didn't know what to think. Then her lips twitched. "Well, maybe at some point I would have, it's hard to tell. Maybe you'd have turned out to have some obnoxious character trait that I simply couldn't handle."

He fought to keep from smiling. "You think?"

He watched her fight to keep the humor in their banter, but the toll suddenly became too great. She shook her head and her bottom lip trembled. Ever so slightly, but visible nonetheless.

He was out of the chair like a bullet and around the desk she'd kept between them. Barricades be damned. He pulled her up from the chair by her shoulders, turned her to face him. "Do you feel this," he asked her, trying like hell not to sound as desperate as he felt, "between us, this...this—"

"Yes," she breathed. "But, Sean, I can't—"

"You can. Let me help you, Laurel. Let me be there for you." He leaned down, brushed his lips over hers. She didn't return the kiss, but her shuddering response told him enough. He looked back into her eyes. "Do you have anybody there for you? Anyone you're turning to?"

She simply stared at him and that was answer enough.

"Let me. I'm a big boy, I can handle the consequences."

Her breath came out in a little laugh, then hitched. "That's just it, I'm not sure *I* can."

He tilted her chin up. "I'm not going anywhere."

"It's going to get—I couldn't guarantee—" She

turned her head aside. ''I'd disappoint you, Sean. If you knew what's going on—''

He turned her face back to his. ''Let me be the judge of that, okay?'' he said softly. Now that she was here, in his hands, so close he could breathe in her scent, just dip his head and taste her...he knew he wasn't going to let her go. Unless she asked him to.

''Tell me you don't want me here, Laurel. Problems be damned. Tell me you don't want me in your life.''

She stared into his eyes, and the yearning he saw there almost undid him completely. What was he doing? What exactly was he offering? He realized he honestly had no idea. And yet the thought of walking away was simply untenable.

''I don't want to hurt you,'' she said.

''Don't ask me to stay because you're worried about my feelings. But don't tell me to leave for that reason, either.''

''I don't mean now.''

''Fine. We can worry about later...later.'' He closed the remaining distance between them.

AS DEEPLY AS SHE ACHED for his kiss, the instant his lips brushed hers, Laurel knew she couldn't do this. Not now. She pulled back, out of his arms completely.

He masked his surprise quickly, but remained where he stood as she crossed the room toward the floor-to-ceiling bookcase that filled the entire left wall of her office.

''I'm not...we shouldn't—'' She stopped, gathered herself, willed her heart to slow down long enough for her to get her head on straight. She turned, faced him. Steadier, but not as steady as she'd have liked. Just looking at him did funny things to the pit of her

stomach. He'd come for her, like a shining knight. She
knew better than to trust white knights, which should
have made her feel twice the fool for trusting him. It
didn't. Not yet, anyway.

"I appreciate that you want to help me," she said
carefully. "And I don't want you to walk away. I am
glad you found me. But I need a clear head to handle...what needs handling. And I don't know if I can
have you around and not want—"

"No one walks through life alone, Laurel. We all
need help from time to time. Sometimes it's the
stronger person who knows when to ask for it."

She stared at him. "You speak from personal experience, do you?"

He stared back, then finally relented. "From obser-
vation of others."

"Ah."

Then his lips curved. "How is it you know me so
well, Laurel?" he asked softly. "Ask yourself that."

She had, a million times since she'd left St. Thomas.
Had almost convinced herself their time together had
all been a dream. But the man standing in front of her
was no fantasy. Or maybe he was, and that was the
problem. He was the perfect knight, in the perfect
dream. And her life was anything but perfect at the
moment. Made it kind of hard to trust in dreams.

"Well, I understand the notion," she told him.
"And you might be surprised to learn I've even been
known to ask for assistance from time to time." He
looked so earnest, she thought, so steadfast, standing
there offering himself up to her for whatever she
needed to take from him. The hunger that ignited inside her was surprisingly powerful. Yet the enormity
of what hung in the balance once again descended

upon her shoulders like a too big cloak that might suffocate her if she wasn't careful. Very, very careful.

She'd become mixed up in something that fell well outside of the law she'd sworn to uphold. She would not drag him, a man who was also sworn to uphold and protect, into the middle of this. It would be putting him in the same predicament Alan had put her in. Asking him to ignore his duty, his moral—and possibly even legal—obligation because of whatever feelings he might have for her.

"Are you so certain this isn't one of those times?" he asked quietly.

"It's not the help I'm rejecting. And it's not that I don't want—"

His eyes flashed and she thought for a moment he was going to come to her desk. But he remained where he stood. "That you don't want me? We're past claiming we don't want each other. Neither of us is going to buy that one."

Her body vibrated, the look he sent her was so potent. "No, I don't suppose so. But what I'm trying to say is that I can't...act on that. Not now. Not here. What we had, that was a thousand miles from here, in a place where no one—"

"Where no one cared what you did...or who you did it with?" he supplied mildly. The tone was very deceptive, until she noted the look in his eyes.

And she noted every detail where he was concerned. As if she was tuned into some private frequency that was theirs and theirs alone. "Yes. I'm home now, and while I'd like nothing more than for those things not to matter...they *do* matter."

"We're both home now," he reminded her. "And

what does it matter if people know about me? About us?"

"Us?" It took her breath away, that tiny little word. Amazed her with the impact of it, of how badly she wanted it to apply to her, to them. So much so that she almost missed the tiny flash of hurt that crossed his face at her surprised response.

"Well, I guess that answers that question," he said flatly.

She shook her head. "We can't always have what we want, Sean." Or who we want, she thought, hating Alan more than she'd thought possible, for taking even more from her than he realized. "I'm glad you came here, that you want to be here, and I don't want you to leave. But I can't have you in my life—in that way—not right now. Things are...complicated."

"Because of your recent relationship with Alan Bentley?"

She felt as if she'd been sucker-punched, though in retrospect she didn't know why she was surprised that he knew about Alan. God knows it was almost impossible not to know with the media breathing down her neck. "It wasn't recent. And it wasn't a relationship. It takes two people to make one of those."

"A fact I'm well aware of at the moment."

She stopped, caught up in the intensity of his gaze, wishing he couldn't entrap her like that so easily...yet tantalized by the reality that he could. Almost effortlessly. What she wouldn't have given at the moment to be free to walk right up to him, into those strong arms, into all that promise she saw in his eyes. How badly she wished it could be that simple. Even if it just ended up being some hot, torrid affair that burned out almost as quickly as it caught flame. It would be worth the scorch marks, she thought.

Even as she thought it, she knew it wouldn't be like that at all. Sean Gannon's appeal was hot and torrid, all right, but what they had between them was also a banked, slow-burning thing. If she let herself get tangled up with him, it would be a whole lot more than her libido that would suffer the scorch marks. Her heart would come away branded, as well.

Maybe she should be thankful the situation she was in wouldn't permit her to take that risk, but she wasn't. She wanted it—*him*—badly. Too badly, which was exactly why she had to push him away.

"Maybe the public needs to see you've moved on," Sean suggested. "That would end the speculation of just how Bentley plans to win this case."

Except he doesn't plan on winning it, she thought, the anxiety squeezing her gut. "I'd be insulted, but—"

"I know you have integrity."

Her stomach clenched harder. As did a part of her heart. If he only knew. Knew what she was contemplating doing... She did her best to stem the flush of shame that crept into her cheeks. But she couldn't do that and look at him at the same time. She glanced down, hating herself almost as much as she hated Alan. "I can't discuss this here."

"Then tell me where you can and we'll go there."

Six o'clock. Our place. It took considerable will not to shudder with the unwanted reminder of where she had to go...and who she had to see. "Not...not now. Today, I mean." She sighed, swore under her breath.

She glanced up when he made a tsking sound. His

smile returned. Only this time it didn't reach his eyes. "Such language, Judge Patrick."

She wanted badly to have that rapport back with him, the light banter, the give-and-take that came so easily to them. That is, when stress didn't threaten to eat its way right through her stomach lining. She ached for the flirtation they'd been so quick to indulge in when they'd met, where anything was possible and boundaries didn't hamper everything she said, everything she did. She tried for that smile anyway, failing miserably. "In chambers I can say anything I want."

"Except what I need to hear." He turned and abruptly walked to the door. He stopped just as abruptly and looked back at her. "Did you tell anyone about us? Scratch that. About me?"

She flinched slightly at that, surprised he was allowing her to see how affected he was by her rejection of them as a couple. He struck her as being more contained than that. But then, where she was concerned, it appeared he didn't have the usual controls in place. She didn't know how she was supposed to feel about that, but probably not intrigued, secretly delighted. Not considering she was basically asking him to walk away from whatever it was they could have had. She refused to even think about it.

"Did you tell anyone about me?" he repeated. "Meeting me on vacation? Did you mention my name, my occupation? Even just that you met a stranger who played Good Samaritan?"

From the look on his face—all business now—she didn't think it was his ego needing a boost. No, Sean Gannon's ego didn't drive him. "No, I didn't. Why do you ask?"

"Not to anyone," he repeated, ignoring her question. "Your father? Bentley? A girlfriend?"

Now she frowned. "No."

"Good." He turned then, opened the door.

Ouch? But just as his proclamation stung, it occurred to her that he might have asked because—

"Wait a minute," she blurted.

She didn't think he was going to stop, but he did. He glanced back, expression implacable.

"What's going on?" she demanded, studying his eyes for a clue, any clue, to validate her growing suspicion. "You're planning something." His expression didn't even flicker. She should have realized. *I don't walk away.* His words echoed in her ears as she said, "Sean, you can't just—"

"Maybe you don't know me as well as I thought. Because I can just. And I will just." He stalked across the room. She couldn't move, couldn't breathe. He took her face in his hands, surprisingly gentle in spite of the fierceness of his expression. He crushed his mouth to hers in a kiss that was both hot and unbearably tender. The combination undid her, had her responding before she could think things out, decide what to do, tell herself to pull away.

Then *he* was pulling away. He grinned, and her knees felt a bit woozy. "And I'll do whatever it takes to earn the right to do that anytime I want. Wherever I want."

He made it impossible to think clearly. And clear thinking, she was beginning to realize, was a must where Sean Gannon was concerned. *Good luck with that.* Maybe if she went to bed with him another, oh, half dozen times, she could look at him, let him look at her that way, without her body reacting like a volcano set to erupt. Okay, make that a couple of dozen times.

She struggled to regain the ground she'd so quickly lost. "I can't have you—"

"Oh, but you can. And the sooner you realize that, the better off we'll both be." He walked back to the door and opened it.

"That's not what I meant and you know it." Her pulse was pounding and her skin all but twitching. "You have no idea what you're getting into."

His grin only widened. "I'm becoming more aware of that with every passing second. But did I ever mention that I love a challenge?" he asked. Then he was gone.

Laurel slumped back against the bookcase, catching a large volume on torts as it threatened to slide out and hit her on the head. "Maybe I should have let it," she muttered. "It might have knocked some sense into me."

She clutched the book to her chest, running her fingertips over lips that still tingled, still tasted of him. And while she was worried, about Sean's plans, about Alan, about her father, about how in the hell she was going to get herself out of this mess...she couldn't quite seem to get all that upset about the fact that she wasn't going to have to do it alone.

Maybe it was because he'd taken that choice away from her. Made it not about her being vulnerable or weak. Not even about her wanting to protect him. He'd made it about caring, about refusing to leave when someone he cared about needed his help, no matter the trouble he might bring down on his head.

He'd taken that responsibility on himself. And off of her.

"Blockhead," she murmured...but she couldn't help smiling when she said it.

8

SEAN HADN'T BEEN KIDDING when he'd said he had
some training in how to take care of himself. As part
of the U.S. Marshals' Special Operations Group—
SOG—he'd been sent to deal with everything from ri-
oting World Bank protestors, to helping a multi-
agency task force in a nationwide manhunt for some
of the country's most violent fugitives. Between personal experience, and stories shared with other dep-
uties, what he hadn't seen or done, he'd heard about.

Or so he'd thought.

Not once had he ever staked out someone he cared
about.

He invested himself one hundred percent in every
duty he'd been assigned to, careful to keep the personal feelings apart from the professional. It hadn't
always been easy; he'd been witness to some horrific
things. This, however, was entirely different. His personal feelings in this instance didn't stem from moral
outrage or his sense of justice. Those were things you
felt with your head, your intellect.

He watched Laurel walk across the backwater
bridge, toward the man she supposedly wasn't having a relationship with, and for the first time knew
what it was to feel with his heart.

She didn't run to Bentley, nor did she seem to fear
him. In fact, if anything, she appeared to be angry

with him. He sharpened the focus on his binoculars. Furious, even. Bully for her, he thought. He'd never even met the man and he didn't like him very much at the moment, either.

He wished he'd known in advance the location of the meet. He could have wired it for sound. As it was, he was too far away for even his highly sensitive microphone to do more than catch the general cadence of the conversation. For his part, Bentley didn't seem remotely perturbed by her harsh words and sharp hand gestures. It made Sean wonder at the wisdom in Laurel allowing Bentley to see that he was getting to her. Made Sean wonder if his own intrusion back into her life hours earlier wasn't the straw that had tipped her outside her ability to control her emotions. He hoped to hell not.

He also hoped to hell Bentley didn't so much as lay a finger on her. Sean would hate to blow his cover this early on. His plan, such as it was, revolved around finding out as much information as possible on Bentley to try to put together what was really going on. Laurel's unease about renewing their relationship had stemmed mostly from her fear of putting him in danger. Which meant *she* was in danger. Until he discovered what that danger was, he planned to keep a very low profile where she was concerned. He didn't want to inadvertently put her in more trouble by popping up at the wrong time or around the wrong person.

It was clear, even more so now, watching her with Bentley, that she needed help. He had asked her if she'd told anyone about him, because being anonymous could work in his favor. If no one knew she had a deputy marshal as an acquaintance, then no one would question him poking around a bit. Well, not if he was careful.

He thought about contacting her father, but had quickly discarded that idea as the fastest route to a one-way ticket out of her life forever. Besides, instinct told him that her father was somehow mixed up in this, too.

He focused in on Bentley. The longer he studied their little tête-à-tête, the more he was convinced Bentley had moved past using their previous relationship as a means to get what he wanted...and on to something else. His expressions and mannerisms were not those of a man intent on charming a woman back into his good graces. Which meant this meeting probably involved blackmail of some kind. It was true Sean didn't know Laurel all that well, but he doubted she had any skeletons in her closet, not with her quick rise to power at such a young age.

Her father however...

Sean tucked that away and focused on the meeting.

Laurel had stopped talking. It was Bentley's turn. There were no hand gestures, no overt signs of anger. In fact, it was the opposite. If Sean hadn't just witnessed Laurel's angry gesticulating, he'd think these were two people having some kind of business discussion. Bentley very calmly explaining whatever it was he needed, while Laurel stood, arms folded, listening and not seeming very impressed.

The only obvious thing was that these were not two people involved in any kind of romantic entanglement.

Then Bentley smiled...and the hairs on Sean's arms

stood up. At the same time, the blood drained from Laurel's face but was quickly replaced by two splotches of color blooming in her cheeks.

Sean's grip tightened, but he remained where he was. He didn't think Laurel was in any imminent danger, at least not physically. No, Bentley needed her for something. And since it didn't appear to be sexually oriented, it was Sean's guess that it must be legally oriented, since that was their only other common denominator.

Specifically, the Rochambeau case. Which meant Bentley needed Judge Patrick in his pocket...and had something he could hold over her head. Something, judging by the desolate look on her face, that was working.

Sean hadn't yet had time to research the case, but it was hard not to be familiar with the basics, as the case had been one of the top news stories blaring from every radio and newsstand over the past several weeks. And from what he'd heard, the parish D.A. seemed to have an airtight case against Rochambeau. It was for that reason the media was pouncing on the juicy tidbit about their possible past relationship with such glee. It gave them something to talk about since it didn't seem likely that Rochambeau was going to wiggle out of the noose this time. Which begged the question...what did Alan need Laurel's help for? If he had the guy dead to rights, it should be a cakewalk.

There had been some speculation over what this would mean to the rest of the "family." Bentley had been asked if he was afraid of retribution. He'd scoffed, certain that the Rochambeaus would do nothing that foolish.

Sean had agreed. At the time. Now however... His mind began to spin. Did Bentley have some reason to fear for his safety? And again...what could he possibly expect Laurel to do to help him there?

Sean lowered the binoculars and swore soundlessly. Could it be that Bentley was looking for a way to save his hide by losing a sure thing?

He quickly dismissed that idea as ludicrous. The media had also made big noise over the fact that Bentley planned to use this victory as the springboard into his hopeful run for the senate next year. Losing the case didn't mean an automatic end to his career aspirations, but it would make his lock on the candidacy less of a certainty.

"Damn," he muttered beneath his breath. He wished like hell he knew more, wished even more that Laurel would trust him enough to bring him in on this. Or bring in *someone* in a position to help her. Because, whatever the reasons behind all this, one thing was absolutely clear. Bentley was somehow in over his head with a very dangerous group of people. And he'd dragged Laurel in with him.

Bentley was moving. Sean swung his binoculars up in time to see him turn and walk away. Leaving a still pale Laurel standing where he'd left her, staring after him, looking both murderous...and hopeless.

Sean wanted nothing more than to go to her, to demand she tell him what was going on. But he knew this wasn't the place or time. He wished he could follow her home, make certain she was okay, that she was safe. But it was more important to tail Bentley, to see who was next on his list, to hope for another piece to the puzzle.

He quietly put his binoculars away and slipped silently from his spot. He had a long evening ahead of him, and an even longer day at work tomorrow on what was likely going to be very little sleep. But he knew sleep was pointless until he had a better grip on what was going on.

One thing he did know, he wasn't going to play behind-the-scenes detective for very long. If what he suspected was true, someone was going to have to make Laurel understand that she needed help. More than he could give her. She was going to have to bring the authorities into this—and soon.

But for now he had more puzzle pieces to put into place. He curled his hands and shoved them into his jacket pocket as he headed for his car. And thought how much better he'd feel if they were curled around Alan Bentley's neck.

LAUREL LET THE WARM WATER thundering from the faucet fill the bathtub almost to the brim before shutting it off with her toe. She tried to blank her mind, to let the heat seep into the knots her muscles had become, to settle the riptide of acid that continued to pitch in her stomach, to soothe the pounding headache that hadn't let up in what felt like weeks. Since the day she'd turned to find Alan standing behind her on the water taxi dock.

She pressed her hands to her stomach and forcibly turned her mind away from that memory. Sean Gannon's image immediately filled the void. She pictured him standing in her office last week, offering to be there for her.

What kind of man willingly put himself into the

middle of trouble for a woman he'd only just met? Okay, met, had a whirlwind romance with, including some amazing time in bed together.

What made it truly odd, she was forced to admit, was that she actually understood it. The attraction anyway, the connection. But why he was so quick to court trouble... That part she didn't know. It was one thing to follow up on something that had been so good, but at the first sign of real problems, most men would have hightailed it out of there.

"Yeah, well, Sean Gannon isn't most men," she murmured, then felt the real stab of heartache. Why now? she silently asked the fates. Why send him to me now, at the worst possible time in my life?

I'll do whatever it takes to earn the right to do that, anytime I want. Wherever I want.

She sighed deeply, remembering those words... that kiss. She felt so ragged and emotionally spent. Maybe if she could just get to sleep at night, she could think more clearly, figure out a solution to all this, so she would be free to pursue the relationship Sean wanted with her. One she wanted for herself.

She sipped her wine, then closed her eyes and leaned back again. What was he doing right this minute? He'd left her office, obviously with some intent on helping her, whether she wanted his help or not. She'd spent the past week wondering when he'd pop up again, half relieved, half disappointed when another day ended with no contact.

Maybe he'd come to his senses and run screaming from the disaster—the very public disaster—her life was rapidly becoming. She groaned and sank further into the steaming water.

She thought again about contacting her father, asking for an explanation. Surely there was some reason he'd done what he'd done, made the decisions he'd made. Her father, who held the law in the highest possible esteem. And there was the real conflict...how could she knowingly thwart the very laws her father so cherished, that she'd been raised to cherish, that she worked so hard to uphold? Even if she was doing it for his sake.

She massaged the insistent throbbing in her temples. If she'd brought this dilemma to her father, claiming it was the problem of a friend, she knew exactly what his recommendation would be. Go to the police, do whatever was necessary to bring the lying, cheating bastards to justice. The hell with ruined reputations and public scandal. If they hadn't wanted to deal with that eventuality, then they shouldn't have muddied their own waters to begin with.

She could hear the words as plainly as if he were standing right beside her. Tried to envision herself standing in front of him, asking him if he'd muddied his own waters...and what could possibly have driven him to do it.

She sat up suddenly, sloshing water over the side of the tub, not caring. Enough was enough. Alan had given her just enough proof to have her doubting her own father, the one man she'd always known she could trust above all others. Furious all over again, at Alan and her father, she climbed out of the tub, wrapped a towel around her dripping-wet body and stalked from the bathroom. She had to do something, had to find some way to either exonerate her father, to prove he hadn't done anything wrong...or to find something equally devastating to hold over Alan's head.

She rubbed her skin so hard it turned pink as her mind skated once again over every possible avenue and path. Of course, the obvious answer was to threaten to go to the press with Alan's behind-the-scenes involvement with the Rochambeau family, with his blackmail scheme, with his plans to keep his name above reproach so he could climb the political ladder. Snake. If she'd had actual proof, which she didn't, she could go to the police, as well.

Of course she'd threatened him with that very thing this afternoon.... She shuddered as she remembered his very calm reply. He'd made it clear that he wasn't going to be the only one disappointed in her if she did that. He'd also made it clear that the other party didn't play as nice as Alan Bentley. Bentley only planned on keeping Seamus Patrick from running for his spot on the senatorial ballot. The Rochambeaus, on the other hand, might simply prefer to keep Seamus Patrick from doing anything. Permanently.

Shaking, feeling nauseous all over again, she pulled a robe tightly around her and walked over to the desk where she'd left the mini-cassette tape. She picked it up, turned it over in her hands. Her conversation with Alan from a week ago had recorded fairly clearly. She only wished Alan had done more than make veiled threats. It was a little, but it wasn't enough. And even if she had enough, she wasn't sure what she'd do with it. It wasn't just her father's reputation or his future career at stake. It was possibly his very life.

She walked over to her dresser and opened the top drawer, took out the small locked jewelry box that held the pieces she'd inherited from her mother and her grandmother. She slipped the tape inside, then shoved the whole thing back in the drawer. Shame. That was what she was feeling, she realized. For her cowardice and her inability to figure out a solution to this mess, a solution that only punished the villains, without taking down any of the good guys in the process.

She sank down onto her bed, staring at herself in her dresser mirror. "You learned a long time ago that the world isn't separated into the black hats and the white hats." There were a lot of gray hats out there, just to confuse things.

Her phone rang, making her jump. She glanced at the clock. It was after ten. Who could be calling her at this hour? She didn't have any cases pending that warranted late-night calls.

Except one.

Her skin crawled with dread as the phone rang again. She debated letting her machine pick up, but knew it was better to just get it over with. She snatched the receiver up on the third ring. "Yes?" she said, her tone edgy with wariness and fatigue. And maybe a little resentment. When this was all over, she thought, she was going back to St. Thomas for an extended vacation, and to do some serious thinking about her future.

Visions of lying on white sandy beaches switched her mind back to Sean. So it took her a moment when he spoke into her ear for her to determine that she wasn't merely fantasizing.

"I'm sorry to call you so late."

"Sean?"

"I need to talk to you."

Her heart was drumming loudly, her entire body tightening against the need to reach out to him, to pour her heart out, to beg him to come help her out of this mess...or just to hold her while she worked her own way through it. "I don't think that's a good idea," she said, biting her lip against the sudden pressure behind her eyes. "It's late."

"*You* need to talk to *me*, Laurel," he said. His tone was flat, no indication if this was a personal call or—

"Why?" she asked warily. "What have you been up to?" She assumed he'd given up on whatever little plan he'd hatched that day in her office. She knew he had a full-time job out at Beauregard, a new job that would surely be demanding of his time and energy. Why in the hell would he spend whatever time he had left on a woman who'd made it clear she was more trouble than she was worth?

As with all the other times she'd asked herself that question, no answer came to mind.

"It doesn't have to be tonight. Maybe we could set something up for tomorrow."

She frowned now. "What is this about, Sean?"

"I'd really rather not talk about it over the phone."

"If it's about us seeing each other, I appreciate your persistence," she said. More than he could know, she thought. He was the only good thing she had going at the moment, even if she couldn't do anything about it. "But until this trial is over, I really can't—"

"It's not about that—or not directly anyway."

His tone was all business, with a clear thread of agitation running through it. Not the charming man who wanted to seduce her, or the intense man who wanted to make her understand how important their chance meeting in St. Thomas had become to him. This was...this was a whole new side to Sean Gannon. She suspected this was the Marshal side. And it made her sit up straighter, made her clutch the phone a bit more tightly. "I need you to tell me what this is about."

"Meet me tomorrow. You pick the place. Preferably not somewhere you'd normally be seen."

Now he was beginning to scare her. "Sean—"

"Laurel, please."

It was that slight bending, the personal concern that filtered in, that pushed her past the boundaries of common sense. But what the hell, she was already so far out on the edge in every other way, why not, right? "I'm never going to be able to sleep now. Why don't you come here? Now. Tonight." She tried to keep her body from clamoring at the very idea of having Sean, alone, with a bedroom in close proximity, and nowhere to be for several hours.

There was a long pause.

"I don't want to be out this late. If it's that important, you can come to me," she said, her body clamoring anyway. Not that she was going to do anything about it. But damn if she didn't want to. Just a few hours of blissful escape from reality. Except when it was over, everything would just be that much more complicated. And things were complicated enough at the moment. "Do you need directions?"

"No. Go downstairs and unlock your back door."

"How do you know I'm upst—" But he'd hung up.

She gripped her bathrobe closer and crept down the stairs and down the short hallway to her kitchen,

which was in the rear of her small two-bedroom
home. Through the dark shadows of her kitchen she
could make out the upper half of a man standing just
beyond the sheer curtains on the other side of her
back door.

Sean.

9

LAUREL TIGHTENED THE BELT of her bathrobe and went to unlock the back door. The robe was heavy fleece and covered her from neck to ankle, and yet as Sean moved past her into her kitchen, she was acutely aware of how naked she was beneath it.

She should probably have steered him into the living room, but somehow it seemed wiser to stay here, in the more utilitarian, sterile surroundings of the kitchen. She flipped the small light on over the sink, not up to the intrusion of the overhead lighting. She motioned to the small round table in the center of the room. "Would you like some coffee? I'd be glad to make some while you explain what the hell you were doing outside my house at midnight."

Her testy tone brought a hint of a smile to his otherwise very serious expression. "Yes, thanks. Black would be fine." He sat at her table, and it struck her how big he was as he angled his chair so he could stretch out his legs.

She turned her back to him, getting the makings of coffee from the cupboard. It didn't matter in the least how imposing he was, she told herself. Nor was she going to imagine what he'd look like, sprawled naked across her queen-size bed. She didn't have to. She already knew exactly what he looked like sprawled naked in bed. God. "Go ahead," she instructed him. "I'm listening."

"I've done some poking around."

She stopped in midscoop, then willed herself to continue. She felt his gaze on her, knew he hadn't missed her telltale pause. But there was no need to let him see how much he affected her, or how seriously his intrusion in her life could affect her. "Have you?" she said, striving for a conversational tone.

"Laurel, the gig's up. I know what's going on."

She did stop now, wishing her heart hadn't begun to race. Her palms began to sweat. She wasn't sure if it was fear for herself or for what she'd unwillingly dragged him into. Both, she decided. Carefully concealing that fear, or so she hoped, she turned to face him.

He really was imposing. Maybe it was the casual clothes. She realized she'd never seen him in jeans and a T-shirt before. If she wasn't so damn preoccupied by the constant strain, she'd have laughed at the realization that, no, she'd pretty much only seen him in work clothes...and naked.

And somehow the T-shirt that hung on all the right muscles, the jeans that molded themselves to his thighs so casually she knew he'd worn them many times before, painted an image in her mind even sexier than the one of him in bed. Or at least an image just as sexy.

She shook those thoughts from her mind. This wasn't about them, wasn't about their relationship, former or future. If only things were that simple. Her life at the moment was anything but.

"I told you to leave this alone," she said.

"You told me to leave *you* alone until this was over.

Seeing as how I want to continue what we started on St. Thomas—and so do you," he added before she could reply, "I had a vested interest in making this situation go away as soon as possible."

"You have no idea what you've gotten yourself into."

He sighed then and dropped the defensive posture. "No, you're right about that." He motioned to the other seat. "Forget the coffee. Sit down. We need to talk about this."

"Sean—"

He looked at her. "I'm in it now. I'm not going anywhere."

She folded her arms in front of her, hugging herself. "That's what I'm most afraid of," she said quietly.

"I didn't misread you in your office that day," he said matter-of-factly. "I know you still want—"

She shook her head. "Not that. I know...we both know—" She stopped, shook her head. "Listen, I appreciate you wanting to help me, more than you can possibly know. It means—" She stopped again, had to catch herself for a moment before she became emotional. This was a bad idea. She should have never let him in here this late at night. She was tired, emotionally and physically, and her barriers weren't as strong as they should be.

"What will it take for you to realize that I got into this of my own free will?" he asked into the quiet of the room. "I don't expect you to protect me, nor is my involvement your responsibility." He pushed his chair back, turned to face her fully. "You don't have anyone else to turn to. You haven't gone for help. Not from the police, not from fellow members of the bar or the bench, not from your father."

She tightened up. "What do you know about my father?"

His expression shuttered a bit. "That's something else we need to discuss. I think I understand why you think you can't go to him, but you—"

She held up both hands, as if they would be enough to ward him off, to make him stop saying the things she knew he was going to say. "I don't care how much poking around you've done, how it might look on the surface, but you don't have any idea what you're talking about when it comes to me and my father. This is exactly why I didn't want to discuss this with you," she said, her emotions getting the better of her. "You have this strong moral code." She laughed, but it was completely without humor. "Hell, I always thought I did, too. But things happen, things you can't explain, unexpected things, that you just have to deal with. And suddenly the world isn't black and white. And all the things you thought you knew to be true are suddenly in question. Right and wrong become ambiguous. You might have never questioned the difference between the two before, but then suddenly it's a tangled spider's web of lies, deceit...love and trust."

She turned abruptly away as she felt the tears burn behind her eyes. She braced her hands on the counter, struggled to get her temper under control. "I respect that you think you understand the situation, and I'm grateful you cared enough to want to help me," she began, her tone studiously polite, despite that the ragged hoarseness of her tone gave away how emotionally on edge she was at that moment. "But I'd greatly appreciate it if you'd stop. If you'd just—" Her voice caught, the tears brimmed, her throat closed over. "Just stop," she whispered fiercely.

She heard the chair scrape the floor. Then he was behind her. She tried to pull herself together, but he was turning her around, tugging her against him. She tried to move aside, but he just wrapped his arms more tightly around her, crowded her against the counter, against him.

She gave up fighting him and leaned into him, just for a moment. Just for a blessed moment.

His hand came up to stroke her hair, her back. She felt his lips press against her temple, shuddered at the intensity of her twin needs for comfort and desire.

"You're not alone in this, Laurel," he whispered. "I won't let you be."

She started to speak but he shushed her with his quiet words.

"You're in over your head. Some very bad people are involved in this mess, and Alan Bentley—" He stopped and she felt his body tense, as if he had to struggle with the emotions that name riled up in him.

She could identify with that struggle.

"Bentley needs to be stopped," he went on, his voice deadly calm.

Laurel shifted back a bit. Sean loosened his grip just enough for her to look up at him. "What did I do to deserve such avid devotion?" she asked, thinking to lighten things up a little. Only the question came out too sincerely, too baldly curious.

He looked down into her eyes, his own expression so serious, so intent. "You made me laugh. You made me want." He pushed her hair from her face, stroked her cheek. "You made me happy."

Simple words and yet they made her heart pound.

"I should be making you run screaming in the opposite direction." She shook her head when he started to talk. "You make me all those things, too, Sean. The timing is just so—"

"Perfect," he finished, surprising a hollow laugh from her. "It is," he insisted. "Yes, things are rocky for you. But rocky times happen. I'll have them, too."

"Things are more than a little rocky," she told him.

He half shrugged, settling his arms back around her waist. "We'll handle it."

We. How nice that sounded. If only... "You just moved here. Surely you're a bit overwhelmed with all that's going on in your life, with your new job, settling in."

"A little. I'll handle that, too." He squeezed her when she started to argue. "Laurel, we met and spent some time together. I want more. You want more. I'm at a point in my life where I'm ready for more. Yes, the new job is demanding. But I love it. It was exactly the right thing to do. Yes, this whole mess is a pain in the ass, too. But dealing with it together is also the right thing to do."

She smiled a little. "Has anyone ever told you you're a hard man to disagree with?"

His lips twitched, but his eyes were still searching hers. "One or two."

"So..." she started, a million questions rolling through her mind, a million decisions to be made. "You're liking the new job."

"Yeah, I'm liking the new job," he said, but his attention was obviously not on her question.

She stopped talking and simply gazed into his eyes, eyes so focused on her it made her shiver a little in anticipation. She couldn't help it—she wanted him. So badly she could almost taste it. Taste him. She hadn't forgotten his taste, his scent, how he sounded when he was moving deep inside of her.

Her breath caught a little. "I'm glad you're here," she choked out, giving up any attempt at recapturing her strong, independent front. Where had it gotten her anyway?

He tipped up her chin when she tried to look away, sniffling quietly. "I'm glad I'm here, too. Don't push me away again, Laurel."

"Like I said before," she whispered, "I just don't want you hurt."

"Life doesn't give out guarantees. I could be hit by a falling comet tomorrow."

The absurdity of the comment startled a watery laugh from her. "What?"

"I'm just saying that no one knows what will happen an hour from now, much less a day, a week, a year. All we have is this moment. And right at this particular one, I don't want to be anywhere else."

She managed to unfold her arms, which he'd squeezed between them when he'd taken her in his arms, and weave them around his waist. She laid her cheek on his chest and let loose a deep sigh. The beating of his heart was a steadying sound, the sound of life, of hope. "Thank you," she said softly.

He stroked her back, her hair. "For?"

"Going for what you want. Not giving up just because it's hard. Because it's not storybook perfect." She looked up at him. "I wish it was, Sean. I wish we were back on that island, back where trouble was a thousand miles away and—"

He silenced her then with a kiss. And there was nothing calm or steady about it. It was fierce and hot and it literally stole her breath. And a good piece of her heart.

She should fight him, fight this, but she had about as much chance of fighting the entire Rochambeau family as she did her need for him, for this, right now. Her arms went around him, fingers clutching at his hair, body pushing into his, wanting to be absorbed by him. Wanting her need for him to obliterate all the rest of it, all the things she couldn't control, the things she was afraid were going to happen, the things she didn't want to know.

It was Sean who tore his mouth away first. "Dammit, Laurel."

She stiffened. "What did I do?"

He framed her face, his fingers pushing into the tangle her hair had become, his gaze so intent on her she felt physically branded by it. "You're like some...I don't know, a drug or something. You're in my system and I can't get you out of it." He tightened his grip when she would have spoken. "And I don't want to. Do you understand?" He blew out a breath on a laugh, but there was no humor in it. "And if you do, explain it to me." He looked back at her. "It's insane how much I want you, how badly I need this." He kissed her again.

And despite the alarm his words ignited inside her, she responded instantly. He groaned deep in his throat as she took the kiss deeper. When she moaned, whatever was left of his control snapped. His hands moved then, traveling down her arms, up her torso. Laurel squirmed, shifted closer to him, wanting nothing more than to rip her bathrobe off so she could feel those strong, questing hands directly on her flesh.

His mouth left hers, traveled in a rough, wet path

along her jaw, making her gasp as he moved lower still. He pressed her back against the counter, pulling her robe open as he continued all but devouring her. With his mouth, his tongue, his fingers. It was as though he was consumed with need for her...and she was completely willing to allow him to feast until he was sated.

The tiny part of rational thought that was left was screaming at her to stop, to talk to him, to figure out what in the hell they were doing before they did it, before it was too late. But as he shoved off her bathrobe and gripped her hips, put her on the counter even as she was grabbing for the waistband of his jeans, she knew she was well beyond worrying about how this was going to complicate things come morning. Hell, what was one more complication at this point? At least this one came with something in it for her.

And then he was grabbing her legs, wrapping them around his waist as he yanked her up against him, drove into her with a low, growling thrust. She accepted it, accepted him, with a growl of her own, locking her ankles tight to keep him deep inside her, gripping his shoulders as they both bucked and drove each other quickly to the edge...and then over.

She slumped against his chest and he gathered her close, buried his face in her hair, in the crook of her neck. Both of them were breathing hard. Laurel was trying to get her head to stop spinning.

"Jesus," Sean whispered raggedly. "I'm sorry."

She pushed his head back. "Are you?"

He looked up at her, his expression somewhat thunderstruck. "I've never done that, never lost control like that."

"I wasn't exactly fighting you."

"Did I hurt you?"

She smiled. "I wasn't screaming because I was in pain."

She saw the first twitch of a smile tease the corners of his mouth. "No?"

She shook her head. "No," she said softly, then caressed his face as his smile faded and his gaze became more serious. "I wanted this as much as you did." She stroked her fingers over his lips. "I missed you, too."

His breath hitched a little. "Don't even think about sending me away again."

"You wouldn't listen anyway. For a guy who's trained to take orders, you seem to be much more comfortable giving them. At least where I'm concerned."

"I don't want to see you hurt," he said by way of explanation.

And as much as Laurel wanted to believe she could handle this new development, this renewed relationship with him, wanted to believe she could keep it in perspective while she dealt with the rest of it...she doubted very much that Sean would allow her to compartmentalize things.

He proved it by his next words. "I know this complicates things," he said, his tone gentler, despite still being a bit raw. "For that I'm sorry."

"Me, too," she said. "I wish it was simpler."

He kissed her. A gentle, soft kiss that undid what little of her heart she still commanded. "Life is never simple. That's what makes it interesting." Then he smiled and, as ridiculous as it seemed, she suddenly felt as if there was hope.

"I, uh—" She stopped, cleared the sudden tightness from her throat. "I know I kept you out of this, wanted to keep you out of this. So I just thought you should also know that...well, that a part of me is glad you don't take orders well. Glad I don't have to do this alone." She talked over his attempted reply. "But I'm going to warn you now. I don't take orders well, either. And there will be things about this...ordeal, that I'm not going to be flexible about. I know we have this...this..."

"Connection." He stated it easily, certainly, leaving no room for doubt.

"Yes. I don't claim to understand it, but I don't want to run from it, either."

His responding smile made her body tingle all over again.

"But, connection or not, you don't know my past, or what drives me."

"Isn't that what a relationship is all about? Learning about each other?"

"Definitely, but—"

"I know what you're going to say. That because this relationship, intensity notwithstanding, is relatively new, I'm not going to understand what drives you to make the decisions you make. And you're right. I won't. Not always, anyway. We'll butt heads. You also don't know what I've done, what I've seen, in my personal and, more importantly, in my professional life, the things that drive me to want you to handle things a certain way. Which is why I'll want you to tell me, help me understand your choices. And I'll try to do the same."

"And if we can't agree?" She knew what she was asking was unfair. She was asking for a commitment, at least temporarily, from a man who was already far more committed than she had any right to hope for, much less expect.

"Then we get mad at each other. Argue a little. And have great make-up sex."

His answer, so seriously delivered, took a moment to process. She let out a little surprised laugh. "Oh, is that how you see things going?"

"Let's just say a guy can't be too hopeful."

She could have pressed, could have forced a more serious discussion, but she knew they'd be having enough of those in the immediate future as it was. But there was one thing she had to say now, before they went any further. "I'll keep that in mind," she said, then turned more serious herself. "Sean—"

He sighed, pleasantly so.

"What?" she asked, confused.

"Nothing. I just like hearing you say that."

She laughed a little, surprised.

"What? Guys like that stuff, too."

"Well, yeah, but most guys don't usually admit it."

He leaned in, kissed her quick, hard and fast. When he lifted his head, his eyes were glittering, his teeth a white gleam in the dim lighting. "I'm not most guys."

Laurel smiled, a bit breathless. He did that to her, took her breath away. She supposed she was going to have to get used to that. "I'm learning that." Her smile grew. "And liking it, by the way."

"I'll keep that in mind."

"You do that." Something inside her relaxed then, maybe that last part that she was still holding in reserve. He made her feel...safe. "And I want you also to know that, if at some point this is too much for you, I'll understand if you want to walk away."

He opened his mouth to refute, but when she just

looked at him, he finally closed his mouth and simply nodded.

"Okay. Now on to the important things." She slipped her arms over his shoulders. "What time do you have to be at work tomorrow?"

He smiled as he tugged her closer. "The rest of my stuff is being trucked down from Denver tomorrow. A friend of mine is bringing it in."

"Some friend."

"Yeah, Derek is a good guy. I hope you'll get to meet him at some point."

She felt as though she'd been living in some kind of surreal suspense novel for weeks now. So hearing him talk about such mundane, everyday things was more comforting than she'd expected. "I'd like that."

"So, I'll be unloading stuff most of the day. I have the day off."

"Then you'll need rest, to conserve your strength. For unpacking."

He slid his hands down her legs, tucked them behind him again, and lifted her off the counter. "Actually, I have family coming in to help me. So I don't need to conserve all that much strength."

"Hmm."

"Hmm."

"Still, it's late, and I don't think you should be driving home."

"You don't."

"Absolutely not."

"We still need to talk—"

Laurel pressed her fingers to his lips. "Later."

"Later?"

"Much."

He smiled. "Promise?"

"About the talk, or about it being much later?"

He thought about it for a split second. "Both."

She held on more tightly as he swung her around and walked them both toward the kitchen door. She thought about the giant step she was taking, having him sleep in her bed, waking up to him tomorrow morning.

Because once Sean Gannon got into her bed... would she ever want him to leave?

"Promise," she said.

10

SEAN DUMPED OUT the coffee from the night before and set about brewing a new pot. He could hear the shower running overhead and smiled to himself. Quite the domestic little picture they painted this morning. Then again, after last night, behaving in a more domestic fashion might not be a bad idea.

Any plans he'd had to take her to bed, to comfort her, to be there for her, and eventually to talk to her about the situation she was in, vanished the instant they hit the sheets. The interlude in the kitchen proved to be foreplay, not the finale. They'd all but devoured each other. And had a damn fine time doing it, too.

Now it was the morning after and he had to figure out how to handle the next step. He had no earthly clue. He'd never exactly involved himself in a woman's life the way he had insinuated himself into Laurel's. He'd also never cared about staying involved, either. He did now. Last night had only underscored what he already suspected, what he already knew…that the only way he was walking out of Laurel's life was if she walked out of his first.

He rattled around in the lower cabinets, looking for a pan big enough to scramble some eggs in, and wished he had a better idea of just how he was going to help her…while keeping her from doing just that.

"Morning," came her low voice from the doorway.

He'd been so caught up in his musings he hadn't heard the shower shut off. He turned and felt as though he'd been poleaxed. She stood in the doorway, hair damp and curling against flushed skin, wearing nothing more than a black T-shirt. His, he realized, as his heart took another direct hit. As he crossed the room toward her, he wondered how many mornings he'd have to wake up to her before that feeling diminished. He wanted the opportunity to find out. "Morning," he said, reaching for her as if he had every right to...praying like hell she wouldn't pull away, make him beg. Which he was pretty sure he would do if necessary. And looking at how the ancient black cotton caressed her damp skin, he wasn't entirely sure he'd mind all that much.

She moved easily into his arms, slipped hers around his neck, then smiled up at him. His heart did a double flip...then went into free fall. He didn't even try to pad the landing.

"You look...mouth-watering," he said. "And I'm starving."

She tipped up on her toes and kissed him. "Me, too."

"The hell with scrambled eggs, then." He went to scoop her up in his arms, but she sidestepped him without completely letting him go.

"Uh-uh. I have to be at the courthouse in less than an hour, and I believe you have some furniture to unload."

"Well, I don't believe I can leave until I'm properly dressed, and somehow I'm missing a shirt."

She dragged her hands down his bare chest. "Imagine that."

"You're killing me, here. You know that."

"I'm a judge, we believe in fairness."

"Ah."

She slipped from his arms. "Is that fresh coffee I smell? If that tastes half as good as it smells, I might have to keep this shirt, just to make sure you never leave."

"Don't tempt me," he said under his breath as she crossed over to the stove. "I was going to make some eggs. How do you like yours?"

"Well, I like them to actually be in my refrigerator first, which they aren't at the moment." She smiled. "Sorry, I wasn't expecting company."

"Don't you eat breakfast?"

She laughed. "I'm on that liquid diet. You might have heard of it—coffee, breakfast of champions?"

He smirked. "Very funny. It's no wonder you pop antacids like candy."

She frowned, the levity evaporating. "Why do you think that?"

He poured them both a mug, then turned to face her as he set them on the table. "Oh, maybe it's the half-eaten roll on your nightstand, the equally nibbled roll on your dresser. The one in the bathroom, the one above the sink, the—"

"Okay, okay." She sat and wrapped her hands around the warm mug, shooting him a wry smile. "Remind me never to leave anything lying around when I have a sleepover with a marshal."

He sat across from her, wishing they could just keep things easy and light. Morning-after banter was hard enough, but they both knew there were serious things to be discussed. "Is it the situation with Bentley that has you keeping stock in Tums, or just work in general?"

She kept her gaze on her coffee, taking her time to scoop out a little sugar from the bowl on the table and drop it into her mug. "As most things are in life, that's also complicated."

"I'd like to understand. As much as I can."

She looked up at him, a little smile curving the corners of her mouth. "That's a taller order than you realize. And, unfortunately, even the Cliffs Notes version requires more time than I have at the moment."

"What's on your docket today?"

She eyed him warily again, and he wished she didn't have to do that with him. He wanted her to feel like she could be completely open.

"The usual," she said. "Insanity, followed by overwhelming mountains of paperwork, with a little pressure from all concerned parties thrown in for good measure." She smiled again, but this time it didn't appear as sincere. "It's what I live for. What all Patricks have lived for, for centuries." She laughed, albeit a bit hollowly, and went back to stirring her coffee. "Or maybe it's just my career that seems centuries old."

He wanted to reach out, but he kept his hands on his mug. He wanted her to trust him with the rest, but he couldn't force that. Hell, he'd already barged in as much as she was going to let him. The rest he'd have to earn. "How long have you been on the bench?"

"Not quite two years." She glanced over at him. "Didn't that pop up in your research?"

He held her gaze unabashedly. She was going to have to figure out that she wasn't about to intimidate him out of this. "All I know about your background, other than what you told me in St. Thomas about your family tree, is what I've read in the papers. That you hadn't been on the bench long. I don't know the specifics. That has to make you one of the youngest women—"

"Youngest, period. But then, I was genetically predetermined for the position. I guess they just figured, why fight it?"

Again the hint of sarcasm, the hint of unrest. Instead of pride, the pride he'd heard when she'd spoken of her father, of his father before him, he heard...fatigue. Weariness. He wondered why, and if it was just momentary, due to the struggle she was currently involved in, or indicative of a bigger problem. He wanted to ask her, to give her the chance to vent if she wanted it. No doubt she needed it. But he doubted she'd let herself reveal much more than she already had. Not yet anyway. He planned to be around when she was ready, but they had other things to discuss now and time was running short.

"So, you were already on the bench when you and Bentley—"

Her head jerked up and he realized that her weariness wasn't to be mistaken for lack of acuity. "Why don't you tell me how much you know?" she said sharply. "Or think you know. Then I'll have an idea how much time I'll need to explain the situation I'm in."

He lifted his hands. "Whoa, whoa. I'm not the bad guy here. And I'm not asking about a former lover because of some egotistical deficiency or something. I'm just trying to establish basic facts here, so we know what we have to work with, what our options are."

"*Our* options?"

Now he did cover her hand, breathing a silent

prayer when she didn't snatch it away. "Yes, Laurel. 'Our.'" He turned her hand over, traced his fingertips along her palm and fingers. "I know it's hard to trust in me, and I guess I don't blame you. And I know our relationship has been rather unconventional from the start, the timing is difficult because of this situation, and that we'd both rather be back on St. Thomas, getting to know each other better under more relaxed circumstances. But that's not the hand we're being dealt." He looked at her then. "You wanted me to step back, wait for this thing to work through to whatever the conclusion might be, and then step back in when it's more convenient. But what the hell kind of guy would I be if I was willing to do that? Is that the kind of man you want in your life?"

She looked a little stunned by his intensity, but before he could tone it down, she responded. "I guess I never thought about it like that. I was really just thinking I didn't want to cause trouble for you."

He grinned. "Well, I hate to tell you, but you found trouble the moment you climbed in that Jeep."

She smiled. "I seem to have a knack for that, I guess."

He heard the underlying thread of fear and squeezed her hand. "We'll get through this. And I'll earn your trust. But you have to give me a little up front, at least try to accept that I'm only interested in the facts as a way to help you out of this mess."

She looked up at him and all her defenses seemed gone, at least for the moment. "What do you know? And for that matter, *how* do you know?"

He took a short breath, then dove in. "I wasn't sure what was going on, but I had a pretty good idea Bentley was involved. And I figured that the only way he could make you do something you didn't want to was because he had something on you. Or something on someone you cared deeply about. So I followed Bentley and took it from there. I know that he was trying this case, at least initially, in hopes of using the victory and subsequent press to help launch his political aspirations for the state senatorial race."

"You said 'initially.' Why?"

"Because now I think his needs have changed. I suspect that the 'family' member he's trying to put away has other family members who aren't all that happy about it. And they're pressuring him somehow to lose the case. He's decided that you're the key to helping him out there, and that if he can't trade on your former relationship, he's going to trade on something else." He held her gaze. "And my guess is that leverage in some way involves your father."

Laurel withdrew her hand slowly, picked up her coffee and looked into it as she swirled it. The only indication of what kind of thoughts were going through her mind was the death grip she had on the mug.

"What I don't know," Sean went on when she remained silent, "is what the Rochambeaus have on Bentley. Yes, I guess they could just have threatened him with bodily harm, or worse, but he strikes me as the sort who would just use that to his benefit. Or at the very least report it to the police as part of the court case. That's one way to keep breathing."

Laurel shook her head, but it was as if she was lost in her own thoughts. Finally she sighed, then quietly said, "They've threatened him with something more important than his health. They've threatened to ruin his future in politics."

Sean would have laughed at that, except having

done his research on the very aggressive and career-minded prosecutor, he knew she was telling nothing less than the truth. "How? What skeleton does he have in his closet?" He smiled. "Besides you."

Fortunately she smiled at that rather than dump her coffee in his lap. "Well, as you likely know if you've seen a newspaper or listened to the news in the past few weeks, they tried to vilify him in the press because of his brief link to me a year ago—tried to ruin me along with him. Seems Alan makes a habit of finding some way to weasel into the good graces of a number of people at different levels of the legal system in this parish—I'm thinking now he's used more than his looks and occasional charm to worm his way in. Makes me wonder what other forms of blackmail he's presently using and on how many people. But that's another problem entirely. Whatever the case, he seems to find a way to swing things his way when he needs them swung, and while it might border on looking too good to be true on the surface, no one has been able to find anything illegal in his methods." She sighed and pushed her coffee away.

"So what happened? Did someone see him trying to work things with you, after this case was assigned, and put two and two together? I know how thorough the media can be when they think they're on to something, like a rabid dog on a bone. Although even I was surprised by the pictures they dug up." The papers had had a field day with the grainy black-and-white stills, taken from film recorded by the elevator camera in the hotel where they'd been staying. It wasn't anything all that torrid, just the two of them in an embrace, but it had been proof enough of their liaison.

Especially with the helpful time and date stamped right on the film itself.

She flashed him a look and he lifted an apologetic shoulder.

She waved it off. "I'm still not— Let's just say I haven't gotten used to being the center of such white-hot media attention and leave it at that."

"I imagine Bentley wasn't all that thrilled with those photos being splashed around, either. I mean, his little system of blackmail only works if everything is kept hush-hush."

Laurel looked at him, her expression a mix of surprise and disbelief. "You still haven't grasped the depths Alan will go to, to get what he wants."

Her meaning sunk in and his mouth went slack. "He leaked the photos? Why would he do such a thing? It was just as liable to come back and smack him as it was you."

Laurel sighed. "When he realized I wasn't going to resume our relationship—and what little time we spent together all those months ago hardly even constitutes using that term—he threatened to expose our little weekend out of town."

"But that was nine months ago. He wasn't trying a case in front of you then. And there is nothing illegal or even morally ambiguous about two consenting adults spending time alone together."

She shook her head. "No, not then. But if he could prove we were at any time involved in the past, then the public might very well demand the case be reassigned to another judge. Someone he had a better shot of coercing to do what he wanted them to do because I refused to bow to his threats." She let out a little laugh, then shook her head. "Honestly, I suppose I was a little naive myself. I didn't think there was anything to leak. It was one weekend, at a conference in New Orleans. Actually, two conferences. I was there taking some seminars and he was there for some other organization, but our paths crossed on, of all places, Bourbon Street. I was in a little jazz club, alone, just enjoying the evening." She sighed ruefully. "He came in, spied me in the corner, asked if he could join me. The local golden boy. Good-looking, charming as hell. I don't usually fall for those types."

Sean gave her a wry smile. "Glad to know that."

She smiled in return. "I didn't say anything about dark and dangerous."

His smile flashed to a grin. "Ego assuaged."

She just shook her head. "Men."

"I know, can't live with us, can't move heavy furniture without us."

"Hmm. And here I hadn't once thought to get you to move heavy things about. Amazing I've kept you around so long."

He leaned forward with his elbows on the table, propping his chin on his hands. "I guess we have other uses."

Her eyes flashed, and he found himself wishing like hell they didn't have the rest of this crap hanging over them.

"And I guess maybe I'm more susceptible to 'charming as hell' than I thought." Her smile was fleeting, the haunted look stealing back across her face as she picked up her now cool coffee and took a sip. "Well, I knew Alan by reputation more than anything else. We'd never argued cases together before when I was still practicing law, nor had he come before me in the courtroom, but he was making a real name for himself in the district attorney's office. It was no surprise to anyone when he took over the top job."

Sean shook his head. "Somehow I don't see you being flattered by his attentions because of his social status."

"Why, thank you. I think that's the nicest thing you've said yet. And you'd be right. Social standing doesn't mean anything to me. I think it was more the timing, than anything. I'd been on the bench for just over a year, and while I was more comfortable in my new role by then, I had also been around long enough at that point to feel somewhat weighed down by it, as well. Of course, because of my age, my family reputation, et cetera, I was being scrutinized far more than any other justice. The responsibility, however, the decisions, the pressure, is all so enormous and I—" She paused, then waved off the rest of what she'd been about to say.

It wasn't the first time she'd done that. Sean could only hope she'd eventually confide in him.

"Anyway, I hadn't had much of a social life for some time," she began, then rolled her eyes. "Who am I kidding? I'd had *no* social life since donning the black robe. But there I was, out of town and away from all the pressures for a few precious days, and there was a handsome man asking me to dance... and..." She stopped, realizing what she had just said, and gave him half a smile. "Apparently I can't be trusted when I leave town."

"There are a few similarities."

Her smile faded and her eyes flashed with hurt even though he'd said it in good humor. "I guess I deserved that. Trust me, I've thought about that, too."

"Laurel, I didn't mean—"

"No, that's okay. Believe it or not, I've met and dated men right here in Alexandria. And there is nothing remotely similar between anything that happened between us and what happened—"

"Laurel," he said, more insistently this time. "I was teasing." When she just gave him a look, he had the grace to flush a little. "Okay, maybe my ego was a bit more involved than I wanted to believe. Thinking of you with anyone else admittedly makes me... uncomfortable."

"Well, not that it's any of your business," she said, relaxing once again, "but to set the record straight, Alan and I weren't lovers. It was a harmless and very brief flirtation. For me, anyway. I wasn't kidding in St. Thomas when I said I didn't make a habit of that sort of behavior." She glanced down, then shifted her gaze to some distant point beyond his shoulder. "I made it clear that was all I wanted. Alan wanted more—"

"Of course he did," Sean broke in.

She smiled again. "Now *my* ego thanks you."

He merely lifted a shoulder, then motioned her to go on.

"Well, he did want more, but he backed off when I put on the brakes. He was fun to be with, but I wasn't interested in him that way. I assume he'd hoped that I would be suitably impressed with his charm, wit and good looks by the end of the weekend to give in then. I wasn't." Her lips quirked. "To be honest, I was more seduced by the chance to just be a desirable woman than I was honestly attracted to Alan." She blew out a deep breath. "That one kiss in the elevator was the sum total of our physical involvement...and I never even thought about it afterward. It never occurred to me it could be used against me."

"No one would have, Laurel."

She looked at him. "No one but Alan. I even wondered later, when it all came out in the papers, if he'd planned that kiss as some sort of backup." She swore under her breath. "I had heard the rumors even then, but to look at him, all blond and tanned, with a gleaming smile, you really don't want to believe that he's really a manipulative, lying bastard."

"Yeah, I know. But you stood up to him—that's the important thing."

"I keep trying to tell myself that. The hit I've taken in the media has had me questioning that call more than once but, in the end, if I had to do it all over again, I'd have made the same choice."

"Why didn't you recuse yourself from the case?"

She smiled. "A Patrick doesn't back down. If I'm going to handle this position, then I can't run every time things get a little tough."

Sean smiled, feeling pride in her swell inside him. "Good for you. So what happened when the weekend was over? Did he give you any indication he was going to come gunning for you again at some future point?"

"Oh, he was definitely disappointed that I wasn't drooling over his proposition that we spend time together back home, make our relationship public. It took me off guard, honestly. I was having fun, feeling flattered by the male attention, but I thought I'd made it pretty clear it was just two colleagues having a nice time away from the shop. He, on the other hand, was already planning on what benefits he'd gain by having a judge for his significant other. Hell, he was already envisioning the white picket fence, his ticket to a great political future all set as part of the vaunted Patrick clan."

"So I take it he didn't handle it all that well when you called things to an abrupt halt."

She shook her head. "He put on a great show of being distressed, heartbroken, even tried several times when we got home to flatter me with a few grand gestures. But he moved on after I refused to even entertain the idea. Or I assumed he had. I hadn't thought about him at all until this Rochambeau trial began heating up and getting attention. I wondered if it would be awkward, seeing him defend a case before me. But we're both professionals, and it had been almost a year ago."

"And he stayed away that whole time?"

She nodded. "Yep. Why he thought I'd renew our relationship all these months later, I have no idea."

"I guess seeing me pop up in your office must have made you a bit nervous after your experience with Bentley."

"No," she said immediately, then squeezed his fingers. "But having you come after me prompted an entirely different reaction inside me." She smiled. "What we shared was a once-in-a-lifetime thing for me. I don't... I know you know by now that I don't let anyone in easily. But with you..." She blew out a long breath. "It was totally different."

"I'm glad to hear that. It wasn't my intention to make you feel more hunted than you already did."

"No, I didn't think that. Not in the way you mean. Yes, when you walked into my office that day, it was a shock. But I never once compared it to...then. I was so thrilled to see you, standing there, right there, right within reach. I'd thought about you a thousand times. And yet, because of everything that was happening, I didn't dare let myself even for one moment believe I could just let you back into my life. No matter how badly I wanted to." She took his hand, turned it over in her own, laced her fingers through his. "On St. Thomas, you were this wonderful surprise. I was willing to enjoy what we had while it lasted, and I was fully prepared, given the fact that we lived in different states, to walk away when it ended. I wasn't thinking about my career or my future. I was simply enjoying my time with you." She squeezed his hand. "And very quickly I came to realize I wanted the chance for more, and wondered how in the hell I was going to walk away without ever finding out what could have been with us."

"So why did you?" It was the one piece of the puzzle he hadn't found. "Did Bentley send some kind of threat?"

"Actually, no. He decided it would be more... impressive to make a last-ditch effort of a more personal sort. I guess maybe he thought I was vulnerable the first time because I was away from home, so why not see if lightning would strike twice?"

Sean's blood went cold. "You mean Bentley came to St. Thomas?"

She nodded. "That morning after we—after I went back to my resort, he was waiting for me at the water taxi." She squeezed his fingers, almost painfully hard, as she came to grips with the memory.

"He's got a major case to build and he just trots down to the Caribbean on a wing and a prayer?" Sean had to work hard not to say anything else or to let the sudden rage he felt show. Slimy, weaseling bastard.

"I'd already made it clear before I left that it wasn't going anywhere, but I guess the Rochambeaus had him sufficiently spooked that he figured he had to go for broke."

"Just how long ago did he start trying to 'rekindle' things?"

"At the time I didn't put it together, but looking back, it was right when the case was coming together and the D.A.'s office was close to filing official charges."

"When did he switch from trying to seduce you to threatening you?"

Laurel eyed him for a moment, apparently trying to guess if he was asking what exactly happened on the island between her and Alan. He breathed a sigh of relief and realized he'd made another step toward gaining her trust, when she said, "When I told him he'd wasted a plane ticket. I got on the water taxi, informed the captain that he wasn't a resort guest, and left him on the dock."

"You could have come to me, Laurel. You didn't have to leave."

"Yes, I did. I'd only just met you, had just begun entertaining the idea that we might be able to do something with our relationship. But I had no idea about the job offer here at Beauregard—"

"You would have. I'd have told you before we left St. Thomas. Like I said before, I'd already decided to take it before I met you. For a lot of reasons."

"I only knew that you lived in Denver...and the biggest case of my judicial career, thus far, was about to get very, very sticky. Not to mention dangerous."

Now she smiled. "And what kind of woman would I be to intentionally get involved with a man when that involvement could unintentionally get him hurt?"

Sean smiled. "Touché." He stood, walked around the table and pulled her up from her chair and into his arms. "I'm sorry for all this," he said quietly. "Sorry we couldn't just get to know each other without all the drama." He traced a finger over her lower lip, deeply gratified when he felt her body shiver. "But I'm not sorry I gave in to the need to see you again. And I'm not sorry about sticking it out." He rubbed his thumbs over her cheeks. "It's worth it. You're worth it."

Her breath shuddered. "Sean, I—"

"Shh," he whispered, then kissed her.

She moved against him when the kiss ended, pressed her face into his shoulder as he held her tightly. "There's more," she whispered. "A lot more." Her fingers dug into his back. "And I don't have a clue in hell what I'm going to do about it."

He leaned back, tipped her face up to his. "We'll figure it out. I know you have to get out of here. Any chance you'll cross paths with Bentley today?"

"I don't think so. I've got other cases I'm adjudicating that will take up most of the today. Most of the rest of this week, in fact."

"Is there any...deadline? With his latest threat, I mean."

She paused before answering. "I have to figure things out. Soon. He'll be filing motions later next week. That's when it will begin. I might be able to postpone things a bit, but not more than a few days longer, the beginning of the week after next, tops." She shivered again, but this time not in pleasure.

Sean rubbed her arms and linked his hands with hers. "Okay, so we'll talk tonight."

She moved away, grabbed both of their mugs and took them to the sink. "I have to get ready for work." She turned to face him. "There's a key under the stone squirrel by the back door garden. Why don't you take that with you?"

"Okay."

"And if you're not too tired after moving everything in, maybe we can eat dinner here together while we finish our talk." She smiled. "Of course, you might as well learn now that if you want something that doesn't come in little white carry-out cartons, you'll be doing the cooking."

Sean was both relieved that she wasn't balking at them moving forward as a couple and impatient. So what else is new? he thought. With Laurel he couldn't seem to get enough, fast enough, for long enough. "Well, you might as well be warned that my cooking abilities are ranked at about the bachelor survival level." He walked over to her, pulled her back into his arms, already missing her. It should have surprised him, how badly he needed to hold her, to touch her. That it seemed almost critical that she touch him, feel him...leave for work with the taste of him on her lips.

"So, sesame chicken okay with you, then?" she asked with a laugh.

"Make mine Schezuan and we're on."

"Ah, why doesn't it surprise me that you'd go for the hot and spicy?"

He grinned and cupped her backside, pressing her between his legs. "I have no idea."

Her eyebrows lifted. "Why, Marshal, you seem a bit...stirred up."

He lowered his head. "Imagine that." And he kissed her again, only this time there was nothing gentle or reassuring about it. Before his hunger completely got the best of him, he managed to drag his mouth away from hers. "Jesus, is it just me who finds this insane?" he asked, pressing his forehead to hers, both of them breathing a little unevenly.

"Not just you," she murmured. She reluctantly pulled away. "I'm going to be late."

She made it to the door and it took all of his willpower to remain where he stood.

"One more thing," he said. "I think we should keep this—us—under wraps. For the time being."

She paused, looking confused and more than a little surprised. "What happened to proving to the media that I've moved on?"

"I'm going to do some digging, and who knows what else, as this progresses. It will be a lot easier for me, and for you, if people don't link us to each other. Considering who we're stacked up against, we don't need to provoke anyone. This way I can move about more freely."

She thought about it for a moment, then nodded. "I don't like it, you getting yourself involved like this, but okay." She sighed.

"Just until this is over, Laurel," he added. "Then I plan to shout it from the rooftops."

She smiled. "My hero."

"And don't you forget it." He grinned as he said it, but his heart clutched with the first real glimmer of fear. Fear that for all his intentions, he wouldn't be good enough, wouldn't be able to get her out of this.

She was still smiling when she left the kitchen. And he was still standing there when, two seconds later,

his black T-shirt came winging at him from around
the doorway.

He caught it against his chest, then heard her footsteps race up the stairs.

Well, that was an undeniable challenge. He was up
the stairs after her in a flash.

They both ended up leaving the house a little later
than planned.

11

LAUREL'S MELLOW MOOD lasted a full ten minutes after arriving at work. She was already behind and had to reschedule one meeting, though she honestly wasn't all that upset about having to do so. Having to juggle a meeting or two was worth it...when she weighed it against the reason for her tardiness.

She was just beginning to make headway into the stack of files on her desk, anticipating the solid hour or so of phone calls she had to make once she'd gotten that done, not to mention the back-to-back meetings she had scheduled all afternoon, when her clerk stuck his head in the door and announced she had an unexpected visitor.

She froze. *Alan.* But no, he wouldn't jeopardize his case by showing up for a "meeting," in chambers, without opposing counsel present.

"It's your father."

Laurel relaxed, but only slightly. She hadn't seen her father since her early return from the trip. Since Alan had revealed that Seamus Patrick's sterling reputation might, in fact, have a little hidden tarnish.

With a smile that was more forced than she'd have liked, she said, "Please, show him in."

"Hi, there, sweetheart," Seamus said, his deep voice caroming off the bookshelves and echoing back into the hall as he closed the door behind him.

Despite her suspicions and worry, her smile warmed and widened. Her father, so big and tall, always so overwhelming—in both countenance and spirit. And yet this huge mountain of a man, who struck fear into the hearts of criminals and attorneys alike, softened when he looked at her. When directed at her, his gaze was never without tenderness and affection. She felt her heart squeeze painfully with guilt. Looking at him, here, right in front of her, she wondered how she could have ever doubted him. She came around her desk and hugged him. "Hi, Dad."

He hugged her back, a bit more tightly than usual, then set her back, looked her over. "Not much of a tan." He chuckled a bit slyly. "Am I to suspect your relaxation was more of the indoor variety?"

She didn't bother to pretend outrage. Her father thrived on being outrageous. She was well used to it by now. She merely raised an eyebrow and said, "A lady doesn't kiss and tell."

He laughed, nodding appreciatively, but she spied the hint of unease that edged his expression.

She cleared her throat. "Actually, I came home early."

He didn't seem surprised at the news. Which, in turn, didn't surprise Laurel. She might not have seen him since returning to Louisiana, but that didn't mean her father didn't keep up with what was going on in her life.

"So I heard," he said. "I was disappointed, Laurel. I know how hard you've been working. You needed that break. You can't let your work become your life."

"Like you, you mean?" She said it wryly, without rancor.

He had the grace to look a bit sheepish. "I suppose I was hoping you could learn from my mistakes."

She reached up and bussed him on the cheek. "Now how could I do that when you make so few?"

He chuckled, but when she stepped back, she saw the concern hadn't faded from his Patrick-blue eyes. "Was there a specific reason you came back early?" he asked.

She gestured to the clutter on her desk, hoping she sounded natural and confident. Like someone telling the truth. "I know there's never a good time to get away, and I appreciate your help in clearing my docket temporarily so I could get a break. But with the Rochambeau case heating up, I honestly felt it was better to be here. You know how the—"

Her father waved her quiet with a simple lift of his broad hand. "I understand." He sighed, a bit more heavily than expected, then gestured to her desk as he moved to one of the leather chairs in front of it. "Have a seat. I need to talk with you."

Laurel started to speak, then realized she had no idea what she was going to say—something, anything, that would wipe that look off his face. That look that was part dread, part resignation. She felt sick. Had Alan thought to cement the deal by threatening Seamus Patrick personally?

Remaining silent, she took a seat in the other leather chair that fronted her desk, the clutching sensation growing worse. Here she'd been still clinging by a thread to her lifelong belief that her father was some sort of infallible god. Which was, of course, ridiculous and childish. He was as human as she was. But still...she found herself wanting to cover her ears, to hum a tune, to block out whatever he was going to say. She didn't want to know for certain, if it meant bursting her little bubble. Knowing would change everything.

A million thoughts chased through her mind in the few seconds that followed. How was she going to deal with it if he confessed? What if he asked her to cover for him? No, she couldn't honestly believe he'd go that far. *But look what's at stake,* the other part of her argued. Not only his stellar reputation, to be added to the long list of Patrick contributions to society, but also his dreams for the future. He was possibly the only sixty-nine-year-old man Laurel knew who was vigorously looking forward to beginning a bright new career. And she had no doubt it would be as illustrious as the one that had led him to this point.

So what was he going to ask her? And what was she going to do about it?

She took in a quiet breath as it occurred to her that Alan may have developed another blackmail scheme as backup. Perhaps he had something on Laurel— what, she couldn't imagine—but something he was using against Seamus to get him to use whatever influence he might have on his daughter...maybe get him to drop out of the race while he was at it. She'd wanted to believe her father would never bow to such a threat, but she also knew only too well that the love and pride that made her vulnerable where her father was concerned...was the same kind of love and pride that left him vulnerable with her.

"Dad, listen..." she began, then faltered. Where in the hell did she begin?

He leaned over, covered her hand. A smile flickered across her face as she thought how the men in her life seemed to have this need to hold her hand of late. Somehow, she didn't mind it all that much.

"No, let me talk," he said. "I admit I've been busy with my own future plans and haven't been as sharp in keeping up with things down here. I had no idea..." He trailed off, and sitting this close to him, she could see now that he wasn't merely upset, he was furious and trying not to let it show. He cleared his throat and began again. "I had no idea that the vultures were circling to such an extent. Bentley—" He stopped, looked down as if to get himself under control.

"Dad, Alan and I—"

He jerked his gaze back to hers and she saw the muscle flex in his jaw. "I don't give a rat's ass what Bentley thinks he might hope to gain from whatever little stunt he's pulling with the media, but if he thinks he's going to influence a Patrick to step down as part of some grand plan to get a different judge, one who'll work to get him on that senatorial ticket, well he's going to have to seriously consider firing his campaign strategist."

"The media doesn't hold sway with me where my courtroom decisions are concerned. You know that."

His face softened slightly, and it struck her that he wasn't as young and vital as he'd once been. It wasn't something she glimpsed often in him—his age—but she did now. And it made her angry. Angry at Alan for his idiocy in getting caught up in such a deadly trap. Angry at herself for not finding some way out of this mess that didn't affect her father.

"Good girl," her father said, once again patting her hand, before giving it a little squeeze. "I didn't doubt you for a second. Merely felt bad for not coming sooner to lend you my support. Both here in private, and publicly if need be."

Laurel stiffened. The last thing she needed him to do was to make himself more of a target for the Rochambeaus. Alan's threat against Seamus's life had been suitably vague enough that, even though she had it on tape, it couldn't be used as proof in a court of law. She wasn't even entirely certain the Rochambeaus had backed that particular threat...or if it was just Alan making his case as strong and intimidating as possible. But the Rochambeaus were certainly more than capable of causing her father to have an "accident." Enough so that she had to consider the threat a valid one and to keep her father as distanced from this whole thing as possible.

"No, that won't be necessary, Dad, but thank you. For caring. I really don't want you to worry about this." It was clear to her now that he had no idea of the extent of Alan's treachery. Her father didn't even know that Alan had no plan to win this case. He'd probably see it as proof that she'd stood her ground when he went on to lose, albeit he certainly wouldn't be happy to see Jack Rochambeau get off. Again.

Her head began to throb.

"I do worry," he said. "I know this is the first major trial you've presided over, and I want you to know I'm here for you. In whatever capacity you need me." He rubbed her knee. "I'm so proud of you, sweetheart. You've done us all proud, not just myself, but every Patrick before me."

Tears burned behind her eyes. She knew he'd think them happy tears, would have no way of knowing they were tears of shame. She felt like a phony, wishing desperately that she shared his passion, wished her career brought her the happiness and contentment it did him. "Thank you, Dad," she choked.

She stood, wanting to end this meeting before she broke down and told him everything. Before she blurted out the one question she hadn't completely quashed, no matter how hard she'd tried. Had he fixed that trial outcome, all those years ago?

But she knew that no matter what his answer, just asking would irrevocably alter their relationship. She wasn't sure which outcome she'd hate more... knowing he'd done something so out of character...or having him be innocent and realize that his own flesh and blood, the little girl he'd cherished his whole life, had spent even one second doubting his integrity.

No, there was going to be some other way. And Sean Gannon was going to help her find it. They'd find a way that satisfied both their needs. They had to. She was still concerned about his involvement, but he wasn't going to sit back to let her deal with this alone no matter what she said or did. And she couldn't deny the peace of mind it gave her to know she could finally share the burden with someone.

If her emotions hadn't been in such turmoil, she'd have been amused to realize that, somehow, a man she'd known less than a month was now the only person in the world she could trust. Even more amusing was the realization that she did trust him. Implicitly.

"Are you okay?"

She blinked up at her father, who was staring at her uncertainly. She smiled briskly. "I'm fine. Just a million things running through my mind. I know you understand how that is."

He smiled. "Yes, I certainly do. And I suppose I

should get out of your hair and let you get back to work." He walked to the door, with Laurel right behind him. "Things will probably get pretty hectic in the days and weeks to come. You call me for anything, you hear?"

She nodded, reached up and kissed his cheek. "I promise."

"I'd like us to take an evening, have some dinner together, maybe talk things over if you'd like. I have a number of meetings with my campaign people and I'm not sure when I can get—"

"It's okay, Dad. I'd enjoy that, too. Why don't you just let me know when you can get down this way and I'll make the time?"

Finally the last vestiges of concern seemed to lift from his gaze. "Good. We'll do that." He leaned down, kissed the top of her head. It made her feel like a child again. Somehow, that didn't bother her too much at the moment, either. In fact, she wished she was that child. Things would be so much simpler. "Keep in touch," he told her as he opened the door. "And don't let those media hounds get to you. You're a Patrick, after all, and Patricks—"

"Never let 'em see you sweat," she finished with him. She smiled as he walked down the hall, enjoyed the varying looks of admiration and awe that the courthouse workers gave him as he walked by. Then she ducked back into her office, closed the heavy door and leaned against it with an equally heavy sigh. Her smile vanished and her stomach squeezed. She walked over to her desk and fished a roll of antacids from her top drawer. "Letting them see me sweat isn't a worry, Dad," she murmured. "Letting them see me fall completely to pieces, now there's a concern."

She moved back behind her desk as her intercom buzzed with the announcement of her first appointment's arrival. At the moment she'd be happy to just settle her stomach long enough that she didn't feel like she had to throw up.

"WELL, WELL, about time you decided to show up."

Sean shot his younger brother, Clay, a look. "Duty called."

His sister, Isabel, climbed out of the other side of Clay's pickup and gave him the once-over. "Mmm-hmm," she murmured dryly. She fingered his rumpled black T-shirt and motioned to his heavily creased jeans. "And just what kind of duty was she?" she added sweetly.

Sean ignored her—a survival reflex skill he'd perfected early in his childhood—and turned to Clay. "Where's Dave? He said he was going to help out."

Clay rolled his eyes. "Oh, he got stuck with diaper duty so Carly and Mom could go shopping."

Sean laughed in disbelief. "You mean there is something left on this earth that our parents' only grandchild does not yet own?"

Isabel snickered at that. "And I thought I was high maintenance."

"You are," both Sean and Clay said simultaneously.

She merely arched a brow. "Fine, fine, but enough with the avoidance. Are you going to tell us about her, Sean?"

He thought about dodging the whole issue, but he intended to introduce Laurel to his family. At some point. His wariness was not so much due to the current media glare and safety concerns surrounding

Laurel. Rather, it was due to his desire that their relationship first be solid enough to survive the introduction itself. At the moment he was thinking that might be, oh, when they were celebrating their fifth wedding anniversary. Looking at Isabel's and Clay's avidly curious expressions, he amended that to their tenth anniversary. Maybe they could both move out of state.

Had he not been so concerned with getting the massive U-Haul truck unloaded in time to get back to Laurel's, he might have been a bit shocked to realize he'd actually thought of marriage and himself in the same sentence and hadn't suffered even one heart palpitation.

"It's...complicated," he finally said.

Both siblings raised their eyebrows. "Complicated," Isabel drawled. "Hmm. She's not married, is she?"

Sean did register shock then. "What? Do you really think me capable of that?"

"Of course not. I was just angling for the real truth, thinking you might defend your way into blabbing all."

He just gave her a look as his buddy, fellow U.S. Marshal Derek Flynn, climbed out of the rental truck in his driveway. "Fat chance."

"When do we get to meet her?" Isabel persisted.

"If there was a her, and I'm not saying there is, what makes you think I'd expose her to you guys? It would be a surefire way to end up alone and lonely all over again."

Clay just laughed. "If she can't handle us, what makes you think she'll be able to handle you?"

Sean looked to the sky as if to ask "Why me?" then

changed the subject. "What about Dad? Is he coming by later?"

"He'll be here. He drove Mom over to Carly's and was helping David install some baby protection doo-dads, then he'll be here."

"Great. We'll need all the help we can get."

"Yeah," Clay said, observing the size of the rental truck. "A shame Brett and Haley had to go back to San Francisco. Family makes for great slave labor."

Sean grinned. "We don't want to scare Haley off that fast."

"Shoot, she gave another Gannon brother a chance, didn't she? She's already a lost cause," Clay said with a laugh.

Isabel was still staring at the truck. "Just how much stuff do you have anyway?"

Sean looked from her to the truck that his friend had not only driven down for him, but had also helped pack. He hadn't really thought he had all that much stuff. He'd been sent ahead to Beauregard almost immediately upon returning from the islands and putting in his acceptance of the job. His predecessor was already gone and things were a bit crazy getting the transfer of duties before the next training session began.

According to Derek and the three other marshals he'd recruited to help him out, it had taken them an entire day to load the sucker up. Sean had been hoping for twice that number to do the unloading on this end. He was missing Brett and Haley more by the second.

Derek was presently leaning against the side of the truck, arms folded on his chest, a look in his eye that said, "I did not sign on for this." Sean turned to his sister. "What about that hulking commodities trader you were boring us all to tears with at Brett's wedding by blabbing his every triumph?"

She snorted, but the tinge of pink that warmed her cheeks belied her insouciant tone. "Oh, he told me he had a long to-do list and couldn't make it. When I dropped by his place this morning with coffee and muffins, thinking I'd help him with his list so he could help me with this, I discovered one of the things he had to do was named Monica."

"Ouch," Sean said with a sincere wince. "I'm really sorry, Iz."

"Yeah, well, thanks. As it happens, he's not all that happy at the moment, either. I threw one of Monica's spike heels at him. Honestly, I meant to hit him in the chest." She glanced at her nails, a barely concealed evil grin curving the corners of her mouth. "I was off by a little."

Clay flinched. Derek suddenly found the ground very fascinating.

"I'm assuming Monica's not all that happy then, either," Sean said, having flinched a little himself. Isabel was not a woman you messed with. She'd grown up with a trio of brothers ready to defend her honor…and had never once required their assistance. In fact, she could probably teach the Gannon men a thing or two about relationship defensive maneuvers.

Isabel laughed. "I'm not sure which pissed her off more—Pete's performance interruptus or losing the heel off that designer shoe."

"And she wonders why she's still single," Clay muttered.

Izzy sent him the evil eye. "You know, I may not be packing a loaded spiked heel at the moment, but I do have various and sundry other projectiles in my purse that could come in very handy."

Clay raised his hands in surrender. "I'm sorry."

At her continued glare, he slowly lowered his hands, thinking perhaps personal protection of certain vulnerable anatomical parts was more important. He kept his hands in front of his fly even as Isabel stalked off around the front of his truck.

Derek chuckled. "Quite the sister you've got there, Gannon."

Sean just sighed. "You're welcome to have her. We're offering a special deal to anyone who'll take her across state lines."

"I heard that, Sean Jameson Gannon," Isabel called across the hood of Clay's truck.

Derek raised his hands. "Don't put me in the middle of this."

Isabel came around the back of Clay's truck, heading toward the rear door of the rental, but paused right in front of Derek. She looked him up, then down, then right in the eye. "Your loss," was all she said as she disappeared around the back and began lowering the lift.

Derek shook his hands and mouthed, "Whew!" Then with a sly grin and a wink, immediately followed Isabel's tracks around to the back of the truck.

"Another one bites the dust," Clay mourned.

Sean laughed. "He can handle himself. He's had special survival training." They both walked to the rear of the truck as the hydraulic lift began to hum.

"Yeah," Clay said, his lips curving, "but that only covers war, combat, famine and extreme wilderness. Not one of which will help him when it comes to dealing with Izzy."

Sean cuffed the back of his baby brother's head. "You know so much about women, do you, frat boy?"

Clay shot him a patented Gannon grin. "Enough, old man. Enough."

They both laughed, then got to work. As the sweat rolled and the furniture slowly got unloaded, Sean enjoyed the steady stream of insults and invectives that flowed from sibling to sibling. Odd as it might seem to an outsider, he enjoyed it, felt somewhat comforted by the normalcy of their age-old routine. It made him wonder why he'd waited so long to come back home.

Izzy cornered him in the kitchen hours later, after they were all done. He grabbed a few beers out of the fridge, planning to take them out to the small rear patio—the only space left in the house that wasn't cluttered with furniture or boxes—and pass them out to his very tired helpers.

"I guess you got the pack-rat gene," she said.

He nodded, finding it hard to disagree with her considering the number of boxes he'd hauled in that afternoon. "I'm thinking of using half of them for firewood this winter. Unopened."

"Only half? Where will you sleep?"

"Very funny." He passed her the stack of pizza boxes that had just arrived. "Here, you can take these out back." He tossed a roll of paper towels on top.

She set the pizza right back on the small bar that separated the cooking area from the dining area. "You in a big rush or something?"

"No, I just figured the least I could do is get everyone their pizza while it's hot and their beer while it's still cold." He could tell by the look on her face that she'd merely been biding her time, waiting to grill him again. He had neither the time nor the inclination to indulge her, despite the hard labor she'd given him today. The sun was starting to fade and he still had several things he needed to take care of before going back over to Laurel's.

"They'd eat cardboard and drink from the hose at this point, so I don't think you're in any danger of insulting anyone if you take five minutes to talk to your sister. Your older sister, the firstborn, who loves you and is only concerned about your well-being. The sister who gave her all for you today without complaint."

"Without complaint? You should have stopped at the caring-about-me part," he said wryly.

She smiled, but when she spoke again, the chiding sisterly tone was gone. "You have met someone, though, haven't you?" she asked with what seemed sincere interest.

He waffled. He wanted to shout it from the rooftops. While at the same time, wanting to hold it close, to keep it all for himself, to hoard these new feelings rather than risk diminishing them in any way by sharing. Especially with his older sister, who had often been less than careful with his feelings in the past.

Her smile gradually faded as the silence lengthened. And if he wasn't mistaken, he saw hurt flicker in her eyes. He hadn't meant to do that. Was surprised, really, that he could. Izzy had never been exactly the vulnerable type.

"I guess that tells me a few things," she said quietly.

"What's that?" he asked, still wary, despite the tinge of guilt he felt for not immediately being willing to open up.

"Well, if there wasn't anyone, you'd have simply said so, and tossed back in my face any pithy remark I chose to make."

He said nothing, just held her gaze.

She sighed. "And that while you were in Denver we drifted further apart than merely geographically."

"I've been gone from home for a very long time," he reminded her. Since he'd headed off to Stanford, right out of high school. He'd gone from there into the service, and after moving around a bit, had eventually taken the assignment in Denver. He'd been there ever since.

A smile flirted around her lips. "She must be very special to have brought you back home again."

Now his grin surfaced. "I hate to even reveal this, but I'd already decided to come home on my own."

Her eyes lit up. "'Already,' he says. Aha. Meaning there is a woman *and* she's here in Louisiana!" She blew on her fingernails, then buffed them on her damp T-shirt. "Don't be too upset with yourself. You're dealing with a pro here, Sean. Never underestimate my ability to wheedle anything out of anybody."

He shook his head and laughed, actually relieved she'd reverted back to her more accepted form: the tough, straight-talking Izzy they all expected her to be. However, that flicker of hurt he'd spied didn't fade from memory quite as easily. And he wondered if that was a role she sometimes tired of playing. It occurred to him that maybe he wasn't the only one learning some life lessons, making some major changes. He hadn't forgotten that she'd just that morning found her current boyfriend in bed with another woman. Despite her seeming dismissive acceptance of the whole thing, he knew that had to have hurt. If not her heart, then at the very least her ego. He supposed he was as guilty as his siblings for believing, or wanting to believe, that the oldest Gannon child was bruise-proof. He was old enough now, had suffered enough of his own bruises, to know that couldn't be the case.

Maybe Izzy had been trying to tell him that, when she'd asked him sincerely to share something of himself, of his private life, with her. Maybe he should have extended her the same morsel of trust he was asking Laurel to extend him. He'd moved back home to be around his family, to put down some permanent roots.

And there was a whole hell of lot more to putting down roots than shoving a bunch of boxes under a new roof.

"She is very special to me," he offered quietly.

Izzy had picked up the pizza boxes and was heading out to the deck. She stopped dead at the door. She turned but said nothing. There was no hint of the smart-ass, sharp-tongued older sibling on her face now. "I'm really glad, Sean. Really glad."

He stepped closer when he saw the sheen of moisture glass over her eyes. He hadn't been away from home so long that he thought for one second she'd want him to point that out to her, or in any way indicate he noticed. But sometimes you had to take risks. "I'm sorry things didn't work out for you and Pete."

Whether she was surprised that he'd mentioned it at all, or because he'd done so in such a sincere manner, her eyes widened…and grew suspiciously wetter. She lifted one shoulder, tried to smile…and Sean wondered when he'd ever doubted that she was just as fragile and human as the rest of them.

"Better I found out now," she said, the watery tone at odds with the insouciant shrug.

"Yeah," he said. "I guess so."

She leaned against the door frame, tried to sniffle without making it obvious. "So, we ever going to get to meet this paragon of virtue who finally snagged your attention?"

"I hope so," he said, then took the next faltering step. "I meant it when I said it's complicated. You'll understand later. But I do—" He broke off, not sure how much he was willing to reveal.

Izzy balanced the pizza boxes and rubbed the soft buzz of hair on his head with her knuckles, the way she used to when they were kids. Only this time she didn't make it hurt. Still, it made him smile at the memories of all the times it had.

"You've been alone for so long, I know you're not used to sharing private, personal stuff," she said. "Thanks for sharing a little bit of it with me." She smiled now, not so worried that he saw the emotion shining in her eyes. "It wasn't so hard, was it?"

He shook his head.

She laughed a little, then sniffed. "Good, then maybe you can help me figure out how to do a little more of it myself."

Sean barked out a laugh then. "God, talk about the blind leading the blind."

She snorted, too, then gasped when he pulled her into a one-armed hug. "You're pretty special, too, you know," he told her, his lips pressed against her temple. "And not just to me."

She stepped back when he let her go, her mouth open but no words coming out.

Sean grinned. "Man, if I'd only known how to render you speechless, I'd have done that a lot sooner."

She kicked at his shin as he passed her by, but it was halfhearted at best. "Beast."

He looked over his shoulder. "I can be. We all can be. But I promise you, not all men are jerks. At least not all the time."

"Well, good. Since my jerkometer has been a bit off of late, maybe you can direct one or two of them my way."

Sean noticed Derek all but leap off the deck railing to come help Izzy with the pizza, and murmured, "Somehow, I don't think that's going to be necessary."

12

LAUREL'S HOUSE was dark when she arrived home. She tucked her keys back into her purse and closed the front door behind her. Her driveway was empty, so she assumed Sean had gotten caught up in moving his things in and was running late. Or maybe not coming at all.

They hadn't spoken during the day, so she'd had no way to tell him how behind she'd gotten. It had all started with the surprise meeting with her father and had snowballed out of control from there. The only positive part of the whole day was that she had been kept too busy to worry about Alan. For the most part, anyway.

She was checking her answering machine for messages, thinking maybe Sean had already come and gone—it was going on eight by now—when she stopped, turned and sniffed the air. Something definitely smelled…different. Good different. In fact, her stomach chose that moment to growl in abject appreciation. Her lunch had consisted of an apple and a bottle of water, slugged down in between phone conferences and actual meetings, so even the hint of hot food on the premises was enough to make her instantly ravenous.

She set her purse and briefcase down by the hall table and walked into the front room, still sniffing the air. Spicy. Her stomach punctuated that thought with another audible growl.

"Sean?" A glance toward the kitchen told her the room was dark and empty. So she walked through the family room, which was almost completely dark, save for the flickering light emanating from the direction of the stairs. She was smiling as she walked past the couch, slid off her suit jacket and tossed it onto the matching stuffed chair. Her smile turned to a gasp as she spied the source of the flickering light. She'd already deduced candles...but never could have imagined the dozens of tapers, short and fat, tall and thin, crowding the wall ledge of the open stairwell. More candles nestled in the recessed area on the first floor landing.

Her hand was to her mouth as she finished climbing the stairs. Had he really done all this for her? She'd thought about him often during the day, despite her crowded schedule. Maybe because of it. She'd been looking forward to him being here when she got home. She'd expected him to be exhausted, maybe even stretched out on the couch asleep, waiting for her to get home. She'd even thought about stopping to pick something up, in case he hadn't had time. But she knew if Sean said he was going to do something, he did it. And he'd promised Chinese food. Of course, he'd said nothing about candles and seduction.

She paused on the landing, staring at the flickering lights, thinking about his intensity, his focus...shivering with pleasure in the knowledge that right at the moment, his focus was going to be on her. And it made her wonder what else he had planned for the evening. She shivered again.

"Hungry?"

She swiveled around, and found him standing in the doorway to her bedroom, wearing a pair of faded gray sweats...and nothing else. Her heart rate doubled. "You have no idea."

He grinned. "Judging by the look in your eyes, I might have a vague clue."

Now it was her turn to grin. Had she really worried that it might be at all awkward between them this evening? For all her anticipation of seeing him again, knowing she'd likely end her day the same delicious way she'd begun it, she also knew they still had some talking to do. Serious talking. And she'd worried that it might spoil...well, everything else.

Apparently, Sean believed in hedging his bets. At the moment she fully agreed with the strategy.

He gently took her wrists, tugged her slowly closer. The heels of her low pumps scuffed across the hardwood landing until her body was flush against his. Then he tucked her wrists—still in his hands—behind her back and bent his mouth to hers. She arched into him, gasping in pleasure, both at the feel of his mouth on hers and the solid hardness of his body.

"Missed you," he murmured when he finally ended the kiss.

She wasn't sure she could state her own name clearly at the moment. The man simply took her breath away. "M'mm," she finally managed to get out. "Me, too."

"I wasn't sure when you were going to get here, so I kept everything in the cartons." He glanced around at the candles. "Good thing you got here when you did, though. In addition to probably creating a fire hazard, if you'd been too much later, they'd have all gutted out."

She noticed then, how far they'd all burned down. "I'm so sorry it took me so long, my day was obnoxious from start to finish. First my dad—"

"You spoke to your father?"

Gone was the husky, seductive tone. Sean the Marshal had returned. For some reason, it made her smile. She liked the complex mix that made him the man he was. "I did. And we can talk about it over cold Chinese food."

He raised his eyebrows. "I guess we will."

"I can't help it. I'm starving. Should we put these out first?" She looked at all the candles.

He surprised her by leaning down and nuzzling the side of her neck, all but growling in a low and throaty moan. "I've been needing to put out a certain fire all day...but I suppose we should start with the candles."

She laughed, then gasped as he turned her face to his and kissed her long and hard. "Well," she said, breathing heavily, "I mean, how bad a fire hazard can they be, right?" She pulled his mouth back to hers, kissing him even as he laughed.

He pulled her into the bedroom, back-walking until his spine hit her dresser. His mouth never left hers, even as he groped at the dresser top behind him. "Ah," he said against her mouth, before finally lifting his lips from hers. "Here."

Hormones swimming, it took her a moment to notice what he held. A long-stemmed, brass candle extinguisher. "Boy," she said, a bit surprised. "You really do think of everything."

"No, my older sister Isabel thinks of everything. Although I'm going to tell her that overkill on the candles might be romantic...until you have to stop to put each one out.''

''Your sister Isabel was the one to suggest the candles?''

His grin turned a bit sheepish. ''I'd like to say I'm a natural in the romance and seduction arena—''

''You're no slouch, let me tell you.''

His grin widened, making his eyes gleam. ''Why, thank you.''

''So,'' she said, not wanting to fish...but basically fishing anyway. ''Why was your sister offering you seduction advice? Did you talk to her about us?''

He took her hand, as if he couldn't bear to give up the contact—a sentiment she was fully okay with—and pulled her back to the stairs. He talked as he snuffed. ''Not in detail. I—'' He paused in the act of putting out one of the taller tapers, then extinguished the flame abruptly before turning to face her. ''You want the God's honest truth? I want to shout it to the world.''

Her heart did a little flip and she couldn't wipe the wide, satisfied smile from her face. ''But?''

He went back to snuffing candles. ''It's not that I don't trust my family, but I thought it was best to play it safe.'' She followed him down the steps, until the last candle was out...casting them in the glow of the only light left—a small lamp on the nightstand back in her bedroom. ''I sort of ran out of candles by the time I got to the top of the stairs,'' he said by way of explanation as to why there weren't any actually in her bedroom.

''Where did you get them all?''

''Izzy has a fetish for them. She gave me a whole box.''

Laurel felt a little twinge of envy at the affectionate expression on his face when he spoke of his sister. "I can't imagine what it's like having one sibling, much less the fistful you have."

They walked back up the stairs, hands still woven together. Somehow, it was that easy camaraderie that underscored how natural their connection had been since the very beginning. She squeezed his hand. "Although I suppose it definitely has its downside." She laughed when Sean merely snorted.

"One or two," he said dryly, tugging her back into the bedroom. "It's always a bit…boisterous when we're all together. We spend most of our time dishing it out and trying to save face by taking it better than the other one. I'm not sure if you'll ever be ready to meet them as a group, but maybe one at a time would keep you from wanting to run screaming into the night."

She smiled at that, even as she let out a little gasp upon spying the thick blanket and tray of little white cartons and dishes he'd laid out across her bed. Though her stomach protested the delay, she tugged on his hand so he faced her. "I do want to meet them. And I want you to meet my dad. Family is important." She reached up and kissed him softly. "I'm sure I'll love yours."

He kissed her back. "Thank you," he murmured.

"For?"

"Being…right."

She laughed. "About?"

"Not about anything. I mean, you're just…you know…right. For me." He laughed a bit self-consciously. "I know it sounds corny. But when I was moving in today, my sister Isabel was there, along with my baby brother, Clay. My dad showed up later. And...well, going home for holidays is always like this huge whirlwind of laughter, talk, arguing, kidding around, hugging, then saying goodbye. I used to think that as much as I love seeing everyone, I was lucky for being able to walk away from all the emotional turmoil. It's an unavoidable part of being from a big family, and I felt like I'd struck the right balance."

"Are you second-guessing moving back home?"

He shook his head. "That's just it. I'm actually enjoying it. Izzy was asking about you today."

"I thought you said she doesn't know about me."

"My older sister knows everything," he said, and so gravely it made her laugh again. "I didn't have to tell her I'd met someone. She was already guessing inside the first ten seconds, then proceeded to badger me every chance she got for whatever details she could trick me into revealing."

"How'd she do?"

Sean grinned, surprised by the question. "You don't seem too annoyed by her tactics."

Laurel shrugged. "Did she break you?"

He puffed up his chest. "You think me incapable of withstanding the interrogation of one lone female?"

"Only if that lone female happens to be a sister. And an older one to boot."

He grinned. "Okay, I copped to having met someone." He cupped her chin, looked into her eyes. "Someone very special."

She'd been ready to tease, enjoyed how easily they did so, so his sudden sincerity left her speechless.

"Anyway," he went on softly, "I guess I realized that my instincts have always been to keep things close, the classic don't ask–don't tell mentality. And today Isabel was asking me to trust her with something important. She'd just found out some not-so-great news herself and had told me without compunction." He stroked Laurel's face. "I realized that it was a lot like what I'd asked of you, to make that leap of faith."

"So you told her." Laurel kissed him. "I'm glad."

"Yeah," he said, his voice a bit more gruff. "Me, too." He wrapped his arms around her, pressed his face against her hair. "I'm glad to be home. Glad you're here. It's more than I'd ever hoped for."

"Yeah," she said, echoing his words. "Me, too."

She knew they still had a lot of ground to cover, and not all of it was going to be smooth. But her stomach growled pretty fiercely, ending the moment, making them both laugh.

"Come on," he said. "Let's take this downstairs and heat it up."

Laurel stopped Sean from grabbing the tray, pushing him down so he sat on the edge of the bed. She straddled his thighs, then reached down and plucked up the carton closest to her, grabbing a set of chopsticks while she was at it.

Feeling his bemused gaze on her, she carefully opened the flaps, then groaned as the fragrant steam rose from the lo mein noodles tucked inside. He twitched beneath her, and her sense of purpose was cemented. "Still warm. Here, hold this."

He'd been leaning back on his hands, but sat straighter now and took the carton, so she could snap the chopsticks apart. Then she positioned his hand with the carton in it between them. She curled several of the thick, soft noodles on the sticks and lifted them above her head, before slowly sucking them into her mouth.

He groaned deep in his throat.

"Hungry?" she asked with mock innocence.

"Very." He almost growled the word.

She dipped the sticks back in the carton and wrapped another cluster of noodles around the slender pieces of balsam. "Here."

"Uh-uh. You. Again."

Surprised, but definitely turned on by the request, she eyed him as she slowly pulled the end of one noodle in her mouth, then leaned closer to he could take the end of another. Gazes locked, they each pulled the noodles completely into their mouths, then swallowed.

Breathing a bit heavier, she stuck the sticks back into the carton, but Sean snagged them and the carton and put both on the bed, out of her reach. He pulled her down on top of him, pushed his hands into her hair and took her mouth with such unmitigated hunger that she immediately forgot how hungry she was...for food.

He rolled her onto her back, among the pillows at the head of the bed, and began to undress her. "It's like I'm starving," he murmured, "all the time. And I can't get enough."

She arched as he slid off her skirt and slip, then lifted her arms so her blouse could slide to the floor with them. "Starving," she agreed, unable to form any real conversation as his tongue dipped into her navel...then progressed lower. Her stockings disappeared, as did her panties. Her inner muscles were clenched so tightly in need she could barely relax enough to let him finish what he was so intent on finishing. And then his tongue touched her and she felt everything unwind into a hot pool of need. She moaned, opened and soared almost the instant he moved on her.

Her climax had barely subsided, was still shuddering inside her, as she dragged him onto her body. He shoved off his sweats and was inside her a moment later with one, long, growling thrust. "Dear God," he said, forcing himself to hold still, buried deep inside her.

She lifted her hips, unable to control herself in the same way. And that was all it took. He lost his control with a vengeance. She met each hard, pistoning thrust gladly, almost gleefully, no longer sure whose moans filled the air. His climax was punctuated with a long, deep growl of satisfaction, and she clung to him, wanting to feel every last vibration and pulse.

He rolled onto his back, skin damp with sweat, eyes closed as his chest heaved. Laurel curled against his side, pushing damp hair from her face, trying to catch her breath. Even after their panting subsided, they lay tangled together, content to silently stroke each other. She traced fingertips across his chest; he toyed with the ends of her hair.

"I keep thinking," she began, her voice still a bit rough, "when we're apart, that it can't be as... overwhelmingly right as it seems when we're together. That my memory must be faulty, or that I'm just wishing it to be that way." She laid her palm flat on his chest, over the now steady beat of his heart. "So I'm always a bit stunned when it's really all that and more."

"I know," he said, his voice filled with the same sense of wonder. He covered her hand with his, traced her fingers with his. After a long moment he said, "We need to finish this thing. With Bentley."

She stilled, but he kept her hand trapped on his chest when she might have pulled it away.

He continued before she could say anything more. "I know we've been moving along at the speed of light since we met. But I'm not in any real mood to slow down. I don't want to fly under the radar. I don't want to park a block away near a park and sneak into your house like a thief, just to keep the media from suspecting you might actually have a life."

She sat up slowly, looking down at him. "Do you think I enjoy being in the center of all this?"

He held her gaze steadily. "Of course not." He held her hand even more tightly against his chest. "In fact, I get the impression that you're not enjoying much of any part of your job."

She looked away then, knowing she was too emotionally vulnerable at the moment to hide her reaction.

He tugged on her hand until she looked back at him. "I didn't mean to go there. It's just a part of you I've noticed and I can't help but be concerned about it. If it helps any, I'm proud of what you do. But I'd be just as proud of you no matter what career path you took. As long as you're happy." He wove his fingers through hers, tugged her down until she leaned against his chest. "I didn't fall in love with the judge—I fell in love with the woman."

"What?" she said, not quite sure she'd heard him right. "What did you say?"

"I said I love you." He pushed her hair back, tucked it behind her ear. "I want us to be a real 'us.' Warts and all." He smiled and it was such a tender, sweet smile, so at odds with the intense, focused man she knew him to be, she felt tears gather at the corners of her eyes.

"I want my family to scare the hell out of you," he went on. "I want your father to put the fear of God into me. And there's only one thing standing in our way."

"It's...a lot," she said. "A lot to deal with. All at once."

"I know. But like I said before, we don't get to choose where and when life will throw us a curve. There will be more."

"You... You're right," she said finally. "About my dissatisfaction with my job. I'm... I think I make a good judge, but I'm not a great one. Not in the illustrious Patrick tradition. Mostly because I feel too much, care maybe a little too much. Which can be agony in my position. I—I don't have any real aspiration to ascend to the state supreme court. Nor do I see a future for myself in politics."

She'd looked away from him by the time she finished. He touched her chin with his finger, turned her face back toward him. "I don't imagine being the first Patrick to turn away from the bench could be an easy thing to do."

"That would be an understatement," she said dryly. "And it's not that I don't love law. I do. It fascinates me, always has. Mostly, I suppose, because my dad, and his dad before him, were so passionate about it. I was raised with it, raised to embrace the wondrous and amazing intricacies of it. And I did. Do. But...I guess it's taken me some time to realize that while I have a great love of it, I don't have a passion for practicing it. If that makes any sense."

"It does. And I know it probably feels far too late now, but don't you think if your father knew how unhappy you are, he'd want you to do something else? Do you know what you would like to do?"

She smiled, but it was more bittersweet than happy. "Truthfully? I'd always thought I'd like to follow in my mother's footsteps."

"What does she do?"

"Did. She passed away seven years ago."

"I'm sorry, I didn't know. I guess it makes your bond to your father all the more close, and the things you've bonded over all the more special."

She stared at him, somewhat stunned at his insight. "You're a pretty amazing man."

"I just pay attention where you're concerned, is all."

It was more than that, way more than that. He was an astute judge of character and probably his high level of training had only enhanced that natural trait. Still, it flattered her more than it unnerved her to know he'd pegged her so easily.

"So, what did your mother do?"

It was only then that Laurel realized she'd talked herself into a bit of a corner. He'd just told her he loved her. And now she was put in the position to tell him that the single biggest thing she'd dreamed of was someday being a wife and mother. Nothing like a little pressure.

"What's so funny?" he asked.

"Nothing, it's just...well, I don't want you to take this the wrong way." Though she was concerned about putting any pressure on him, oddly enough she realized she wasn't in the least worried about his reaction to the goal itself. Pretty amazing, considering she'd never told her long-harbored secret to a single other soul.

"Spill it," he urged.

"She was...well, this sounds so cliché, but she was the world's best mom. Wife, too, although I wasn't as focused on that part, of course. My dad, however, will bore you to tears with stories about what an amazing friend and companion she was to him. Fair warning." Smiling now, she was warming to her subject...and almost giddy with relief in finally releasing the truth from the dark corners of her heart. "She took care of us, loved us, but it didn't stop there. She was involved in so many things. Everyone knew her. We had people over all the time, just in and out, for a multitude of reasons...and she always made each person feel so welcome." She knew she sounded ridiculously wistful. "I've always admired her, always thought what a wonderful challenge it would be to raise a family, be involved like she was." She laughed lightly, but it ended on a sigh. She looked back to Sean. "Can you imagine me telling my father what I really want to be when I grow up is a housewife?"

Sean sat up, his expression more serious than she'd ever seen it. "You didn't say you wanted to be a housewife. You said you dreamed of being a mother and a wife. You said your father revered his wife, so why don't you think he'd understand, applaud even, that choice?"

"Because I'm the last one. The last Patrick. I thought...I don't know, I guess I thought that somehow I could have it all."

He stared into her eyes so intently, she felt the tears gather again in her own. Only this time she couldn't keep them from tracking down her cheeks. "I don't doubt for a second that you couldn't juggle a demanding career with being a wife, with motherhood," he said. "But you'd probably feel you were shortchanging both."

She nodded, then sniffed so hard she made a snorting sound. Sean's lips twitched and she let out a watery laugh.

"So, don't do it all. Pick one."

She rolled her eyes, sniffled again, even as she scrubbed at the tears on her cheeks. "Well, it's not exactly a job you can sign up for."

"So," he said, helping her wipe her tears away with the pads of his thumbs, his tone too studied to be as nonchalant as it sounded. "If you met someone who filled your...job description, then would you choose it?"

He flashed her a short grin and the words just tumbled out. "I love you, too, you know," she whispered. "I didn't say it before. But I do."

His eyes flared then and they both reached for each other. His kiss was fierce, protective...possessive. And she gave it all back to him as she felt all those things, as well.

"So," he repeated, his voice sounding rough with a few swallowed tears of his own. "If you met someone, and you had the opportunity to do what you've always dreamed of doing, would you step down? Would you face your dad?"

She looked into his face, wondering how he'd become so dear to her so quickly. "Honestly? I don't know. I—I don't know."

"Well," he said, smiling a little, kissing the corners of her mouth. "Maybe we're going to find the answer to that. But first—"

"I know, we need to talk about Alan."

Sean made a face. "I was going to say we need to eat a real dinner. But you're right. I do have some ideas on how to end this thing with him."

"Do they involve specially trained government agents and covert operations of any kind?" she asked warily.

"Nope. Just good ol' human ingenuity. And maybe a little outside help. Access to a few toys."

She raised her eyebrows. "Boy's toys?"

"U.S. Marshal toys."

"Even better."

He grinned. "I just need to know one thing."

"Which is?"

"Ever played poker?"

She looked confused. "Yes. Why?"

"Are you good at it?"

"Very."

His grin widened further. "Excellent. I just might be able to park in your driveway by the week's end."

"Explain."

He rolled her onto her back, straddled her waist...and picked up the forgotten carton of lo mein. He fished one noodle out with his fingers and dangled it over her mouth. "Just as soon as we get done eating."

They never did make it to the kitchen. Laurel didn't mind. As it turned out, cold Chinese food was quite a...delicacy. It all hinged on the presentation.

13

"WHAT WE NEED to do is trap him. Use his own tools against him." Sean spread out an array of equipment on Laurel's kitchen table. "With a few tools of my own to help us out." It was past midnight and neither of them was fully clad, but it had simply taken them a little while to make it out of her bedroom. Neither of them was complaining.

"You mean, blackmail him back?" Laurel asked, covering a yawn with her fist.

Sean grinned. "Basically, yes."

"But won't the Rochambeaus just come after me directly then? Or after my father, as a way of getting to me?"

"Not if we expose their deal with Bentley." Sean knew about the campaign backing now, knew that Alan, in his frustration and desperation, had revealed to Laurel that day on St. Thomas that he "owed" the family too much at this point to find another way to deal with the situation. Laurel had been totally unprepared for his confession, had no way to prove he'd made it other than her word, something Alan had obviously been banking on. What he hadn't counted on was that even knowing what kind of trouble he was in, Laurel wasn't going to be swayed. That's when the threats had begun.

Laurel had been prepared the next time they'd met.

She'd played the tape of their bridge conversation for Sean, and he told her that he'd followed her that day. He'd also tailed Alan, in hopes of gaining more evidence against him. Which hadn't been forthcoming. Sean had also used some of his contacts to see if there was anything floating out there in the intelligence community that might help him, but he'd come up blank.

They were confident they understood the situation Alan was in, and the lengths he'd go to, in order to see himself out of it in one piece...with a senatorial slot firmly in hand, no less. But they also knew they didn't have enough to nail him. Yet.

"If we can prove the under-the-table connection between Bentley and the family, they'll have far too many new headaches to worry about," Sean told her. "Jack's trial will definitely be halted. New charges will be filed—against him and who knows who else. Alan will be in the center of a media storm the likes of which he's never seen before...none of it good." He held her gaze. "And best of all, as a material witness, you won't be trying any of their cases. That's if they're stupid enough to go to trial in the first place. That will be up to their attorneys and the state."

Laurel shivered. "I just hope *we're* not being stupid, thinking we can pull off this whole thing. Better people than us have tried to nail the Rochambeaus and failed."

"Well, better people didn't have Alan Bentley and his come-hell-or-high-water ambitions as their weak link, either."

It was clear from the look on Laurel's face that she didn't consider Bentley as weak a link as Sean would like her to. He couldn't blame her. The man had been terrorizing her for weeks now, putting the fear of God into her, not to mention a healthy dose of doubt where her father was concerned.

She leaned back and let loose a whooshing sigh. "It's all a good plan, but I still don't see how we can prevent him from taking my father down with him. He'll start screaming he was set up and then claim my father played some role in it."

"Why would he do that? The gig will be up at that point. He'll have nothing to gain."

"You don't know him. He'll use my father as a shield, to deflect some of the misery being piled on top of him. Trust me, Alan is a sore loser of the worst kind. He'll find some way to play himself off as the victim in this whole thing. And my father will be the first place he looks for a prime patsy."

This was the tough part. Sean knew he had a battle on his hands. And wearing her down with screaming orgasms ahead of time wasn't going to help much. Although they were both decidedly more relaxed heading into battle. "I know you don't want to confront him about this. But I don't see where you have any choice. Yes, maybe Alan is bluffing about what he's got on your dad, knowing you can't prove there was no foul play and praying on your vulnerability, planting his nasty little seeds of doubt. You said yourself that you could find no proof your father did anything wrong."

Laurel raked her fingers through hair that was long past tousled. "That's just it. You're right. I can't prove he didn't, either. His ruling on some of the motions filed...well, I don't know what was said or argued in chambers before he made those decisions. On paper, some of them were pretty dicey, could have gone either way. In the end, they went the way that Rochambeau's attorney hoped they would. Several key decisions, and he walked."

"So maybe the state's case was weak. Or maybe Rochambeau's shark was just too good at playing legal roulette." Sean leaned forward. "Otherwise, what you're basically saying is that he ruled like he did for some other reason. Being intimidated by the Rochambeaus maybe—"

She shook her head. "Seamus Patrick? Hardly."

"Well, then, that leaves them finding some other kind of leverage to use against him." He looked at her intently. "Maybe they found his weak spot?"

She sat up, folding her arms around her middle, her face grim. "You mean me, don't you? That they somehow used me to get to him? Made threats against me. I was in law school when he heard that case." She slumped back. "I know it's possible but I don't even want to think that, Sean. I can't imagine—"

"I know," he said quietly. "You don't want to. But isn't that the very same thing that they, or Alan in their place, are doing to you now?"

She squeezed her eyes shut and Sean couldn't stay sitting any longer, watching her go through this. No matter how necessary it was.

He moved behind the chair she was sitting in, massaged her shoulders. She was all knotted up. And after he'd spent all those lovely hours unknotting her earlier. "That's the thing about all this, the thing that makes it all so vicious...yet so workable. We can't know what they had on him then, if anything, or what to do about it, unless you confront him."

She said nothing for a long stretch of time. He continued to work the muscles of her shoulders and neck, knowing she needed to sort this out on her own, make the only conclusion she possibly could...and accept it. Finally she sighed and said, "I don't want to hurt him, Sean. I don't want to hurt what he and I have—no matter what his answer is. And I have to believe, have to—" she balled her fists in her lap and her shoulders tensed once again "—that he's innocent of all this. But if I ask him and, for whatever reason, he bears some culpability...then where do we go? I won't risk his future."

"What about *your* future? Would he expect you to sacrifice yourself for his political career?"

She leaned back, looked up at him. "Of course not. But I'm not sure I could live with myself if I was the one to end it."

Sean moved around her then, crouched in front of her knees. "But you're not ending it. If he did wrong, then he was the one who brought it on himself."

"But maybe he had no choice!" she blurted, then shoved her chair back and began pacing the kitchen floor.

Sean watched her for a moment or two, then quietly asked, "You don't really think he did anything wrong, do you?"

She kept pacing. "With my whole heart, that's what I want to believe."

"Are you more afraid of that, or of confronting him and having him realize that you ever doubted him in the first place."

She stopped, her back to him. After several silent moments he saw her shoulders begin to shake.

Feeling like the worst kind of louse for pushing her so hard, despite the necessity of it, he went to her, took her shoulders in his hands, tugged her around even when she tried to shrug him off.

"Come here." He pulled her stiff body close, wrapped his arms around her and pulled her head down to his shoulder. "I'm not trying to hurt you. And I don't want your dad hurt, or your relationship with him. But maybe, just maybe..." He leaned back, prodded her chin with his hand until she was forced to look up into his eyes. Hers were brilliant with unshed tears and it about tore his heart in two.

It also made him more determined than ever to see both Alan Bentley and Jack Rochambeau rot in hell.

"Maybe you need to give your dad more credit. Tell him everything, explain everything. He'll understand why you had to ask."

She sniffled. "I don't know, Sean." She leaned into him. "I just don't know." He heard her silent tears and felt her body tense, trying to fight them off one more time. "If I do that...and I'm wrong about him..." She couldn't say any more. And, finally, the tears won.

Sean wrapped his arms around her again, held her tight. This time her arms snaked around his waist and she clung to him just as tightly. He hated seeing her like this. Hated seeing how deeply this whole mess was torturing her. "Maybe," he started, then stopped. It wasn't what he wanted, wasn't what was best...but he didn't want her hurting any more than she already was. "Maybe we can handle this without Alan's threat against your dad being made public. If we get enough on him, and handle it in just the right way, maybe we can shut him down. And shut him up."

Her hold on him tightened.

He stroked her hair, stroked her back, wishing like

hell he could promise her more. But one thing he knew from experience, they'd both feel better when they were actively working to put an end to this whole thing. Right now, what Laurel needed, what they both needed, was a plan of action.

"You recorded your conversation with Alan on the bridge. Do you think you can arrange another meeting there?"

Her tears had stopped and she'd begun to get a grip on herself. Slowly she pulled out of his arms and went to fish some tissues out of the box on the windowsill. After a very unladylike blow of the nose, which made them both smile briefly, she pulled the rest of herself together, squared her shoulders, and looked directly back at him. "Yes, I think I can do that."

He marveled at her strength. Wanted to tell her then how proud her father would be to see how strong she was, to know her convictions and strength of character hadn't been compromised despite the threat against her. He truly wished he could have convinced her to confront Seamus. He was certain, if the man was innocent, he'd forgive his daughter her doubts, considering the terrible strain she'd been under.

However, that slight possibility existed that he wasn't innocent...and that would not only knock apart all of his future plans...but shatter Laurel's heart, as well.

"What we need is an admission from him about the campaign contributions," Sean said. "Specifically about their origin. If you can get any of the front company names, all the better. We'll nail him for extortion and the rest of those bastards with him."

She sighed. "It's a tall order. Alan's not stupid. But

I can give it a shot." She tossed her tissue in the trash. "Can you record the conversation from where you'll be hiding? I don't think I should take a chance on carrying a recorder this time." She swore under her breath. "I only wish I'd had one on me the first time he made his threats."

"I'll wire the place beforehand. Don't worry, we'll get him. His arrogance, and his belief that he's got you over a barrel with the threat against your father, will make him less careful than usual. If anyone can get him to talk, it's you."

For the first time in what seemed like ages, a smile twitched at the corners of her mouth. "So, are you suggesting I use my feminine wiles on him? Hell, that's what got me into this mess in the first place. And I wasn't even trying."

Sean grinned. "You don't have to."

She rolled her eyes, then rubbed at her arms as if cold. Only he knew the chill had nothing to do with the room's temperature.

"I'll be right there, Laurel. Nothing will go wrong."

"I wish I was as confident of that as you are." She paced again. "We have other work to do. Or I do. I need to find out who we can take the evidence to afterward. I don't know who I can trust in the department. It would be just my luck to pick the one guy who the Rochambeaus have in their pocket. I'm sure Bentley isn't the only one. Just as I'm certain they haven't gotten away with everything they've done for so long without some help inside the police department."

With an adamant shake of her head, she crossed the room again. "No offense, but the federal guys will just make a nightmare out of this. My father's entire career, both present and future, is in the balance here. I want as much control over how this situation is handled as possible."

Sean crossed the room, pulled her back into his arms. "It will all work out." He thought about the probable aftermath, the media storm when the news broke. And he knew it was going to get a lot uglier before it got any better. "Can I get you to promise me one thing?"

"I don't know. Ask me."

"If we think, afterward, that there is any chance that your father might either be involved or hurt by what we're doing, then you have to go to him and tell him everything, so he's at least prepared for the aftermath."

She trembled slightly, but held his gaze, then gave him one short nod. "Yeah," she said roughly. "I promise."

Sean snugged her back against his chest, wishing like hell this was already over. Wishing like hell he could do more to protect her, to protect her father. At least there was something he could do about securing the area where Laurel and Alan were going to have their meeting. "Okay," he murmured, his mind already spinning out all the possibilities for what he wanted done. "Let's sit down and map out a strategy for what you're going to say." He pulled out the chair for her, then went to put on a fresh pot of coffee. It was going to be a long night.

IT TOOK ALMOST A WEEK to set up. A week of sleepless nights and a steady diet of coffee and antacids. Despite the fact that Sean had spent every evening and night with her, sneaking in and out like a thief each time, she was still jittery and slightly nauseous at the thought of what was about to unfold.

She stood in the middle of the backwater bridge, gripping the railing so tightly her knuckles hurt.

"He just pulled up," came the soft words just above her ear, where Sean had wired her hair barrette with a microscopic speaker. "You'll be great."

She made a little snorting sound, but a smile tugged at the corners of her mouth anyway. Just hearing his voice, so calm and steady, was a tremendous boost. It made her glad Sean had come up with a way to keep them connected, even if it did make her a little more nervous about unintentionally giving him away.

She knew the area was wired to pick up even the softest spoken word. She wore only the small mike, which would go undetected even with relatively sophisticated scanners. Not that she expected Alan to have any such thing, but he'd been more than a little wary about meeting her here. She'd finally been forced to tell him that she was going to do what he wanted, but had some additional questions on how to handle certain potential obstacles and would feel more confident if they could have one last meeting to come up with a specific game plan.

He'd agreed, but she sensed this was going to be far harder than even she imagined. All his instincts were on red alert and she had no idea how she was going to get him to let down his guard enough to give her what she needed. *Gain his trust*, Sean had advised her. She fidgeted a bit, stared out at the slowly moving water as she tried to figure out just how in the hell she was going to do that. Barring that angle, her only other option was to spark a fight with him, to make him angry. Angry enough that he lost control.

Sean didn't want her to go in that direction unless she felt it was absolutely necessary. But she wasn't sure convincing Alan that she was now one hundred percent in his corner would encourage him to share any confidences. She strongly suspected she knew where this meeting was headed. She braced herself, took a strengthening breath, as he walked down the narrow park path toward her.

Her thoughts strayed to her father, to his unwitting role in all of this. Perhaps, at the very least, she could get Alan to relinquish more information on just what he knew about that old case that she didn't. After all, with the added threat of her father's life being on the line, perhaps he wouldn't view sharing some of the other details as being all that detrimental to the hold he had on her. Alan was arrogant. That was a character trait she could exploit. And would.

"I was surprised to hear from you," he said.

Laurel felt her knees knock, felt the muscles in her thighs begin to knot as she fought the shaking. "If we're going to make this work, we have to have a game plan in place to deal with the various obstacles we're most likely to face." She kept her gaze directly on his, her tone brisk and totally businesslike. After all, to Alan this was a business transaction.

As expected, he registered a blink of surprise at her superior tone, then a smile of admiration. He believed he'd won. And that she wasn't at all happy about it. Which was exactly where she wanted him. His arrogance had gotten him into this mess...and she was determined that his arrogance would also be her ticket out of it.

"Now that's more in line with what I had in mind,"

he said. "I'm glad you finally came around to seeing things my way."

She lifted a shoulder in an insignificant shrug. "You left me with no other way to view it."

He was smug, almost preening in his victory. "Well, there is that. And while I still see that temper of yours, simmering there beneath the surface, you can hardly hold me in contempt for my misdeeds, or any moral failing, seeing as we both now understand that everyone's morals are up for sale. For the right price."

She worked hard not to give away her anxiousness at the opening he'd just given her. "And just what was the going rate for yours?" she snapped. "Just how much did the Rochambeaus have to pitch in to the campaign coffers to insure a little inside help at the district attorney's office?"

It was a bold move, but he'd opened the door. Could it really be this easy? She worked to keep her fingers from toying nervously on the railing.

Alan's pause in replying only lasted several seconds, but it felt like several lifetimes to her.

"When you sell your soul, does the price tag really matter?" he replied, his face set in stone, cold, implacable.

For the first time she noticed a bit of that haunted look edging his soulless eyes. She was very familiar with the signs, having seen them staring back at her in the mirror every morning for the past several weeks. It wasn't the answer she'd been looking for, but it was potentially damning. A good defense attorney could still spin it his way, though. She needed more.

"How can I be certain that if I do this for you, you'll

keep your end of the bargain?'' she asked, back to business.

"You can't."

"Then why am I standing here?" She stepped back, as if to say he was wasting her time.

His smug countenance slipped just a little. But it was enough for her to realize she did have some leverage here. She'd dangled the possibility that she was prepared to deliver him out of hell and into a rosy future. Now that he'd tasted victory, he wouldn't want to risk losing what he'd gained.

"What I'm asking," she went on, pressing her advantage, "is for some show of confidence from you. That my father will be spared."

"I think I can promise you that."

"And that his reputation will remain unscathed during your campaign against him."

Alan smiled and it made the hair on her arms stand on end. But it was a good reminder of just how evil this man could be. "I don't know that I can give you that. The information I have is too valuable not to use to discredit my running mate." He held up his hand. "And don't cry to me about his sterling legacy. He was the one who made those decisions during that trial. I merely dug them up."

"Exactly what did you dig up? I've done my own digging, as I suspect you know. And while I agree that some of his rulings bordered on questionable, we're not privy to what was argued in chambers, what reasons he might have had for the decisions he made. Unless you know something more that I don't." It was a direct challenge. She held her breath, waiting for the answer.

"I think perhaps that question should have been directed to me."

Laurel spun around, her mouth dropping open in shock to find her father stepping out on the path behind her.

It took considerable control not to swing her gaze to the spot where Sean was hiding. Had he done this? Would he have betrayed her like this? She knew, even in that split second of reaction time that he would only have done it to protect her, because he saw it as the only way to make certain this was completely over. But she wasn't sure, even with good motives, that she'd be able to forgive him for doing this without telling her.

Her father stepped forward and her thoughts snapped back into focus. "Dad, what are you doing here?" She glanced at Alan, but his expression was just as confused and wary as hers likely was.

"We'll discuss your reasons for keeping me in the dark about this little situation when this is all over."

She started to argue, but he'd already turned his attention to Alan. "And you...I'd like to hear your answer, Mr. Bentley." He moved until he was between the two of them. "What information is it you think you have on me? Because I'll be more than glad to clear up any misconceptions you might have."

From Sean's position in the trees, about twenty yards away, he could only see the side of Seamus Patrick's face. But he had clear access to Bentley's. All of which was being recorded on film. He was as shocked as Laurel had been at Seamus's sudden arrival. Of course, he'd had the benefit of seeing him arrive before either Laurel or Alan had noted his appearance, but couldn't alert Laurel. Showing himself now might stop Alan from revealing the most crucial pieces of information they were likely to get.

He adjusted the frequency on his receptor to accommodate the more booming voice of Judge Patrick Senior.

"Just what is it you think you know about that trial?"

Alan visibly swallowed, but maintained a smug sort of defiance nonetheless. "I guess we'll discover that when the campaign begins," he boasted, the epitome of prosecutorial bluster.

Seamus chuckled, completely at ease. Sean's heart began to pound. They were so close...so close.

"Oh, I don't think that will come to pass, young man. Why don't you share what you know now?"

Alan's face had paled slightly at Seamus's heartily spoken words. "I'm not some greenhorn, fresh from law school, Mr. Patrick."

"'Your Honor' will do just fine. It's a phrase you might want to reacquaint yourself with. For when you go in front of the judge to plea for your freedom."

Now Alan drew himself up straighter and taller, appearing grossly offended. But through the scope, Sean could count the individual beads of sweat that had sprung up on Bentley's pale brow. He grinned, figuring he deserved to enjoy himself a little.

"I can't imagine what you're referring to. I have done nothing wr—"

"Has it occurred to you that I didn't just happen upon this little meeting by accident?"

Alan fidgeted with his tie, straightened his cuffs. "I assumed, despite Laurel's pretense of surprise, that she brought you into this." He turned toward her, regaining a bit of the arrogance Seamus's sudden appearance had robbed from him. "You made a grave miscalculation, sweetheart."

Sean gripped the scope more tightly, a split second away from coming through the trees and not stopping until he had Alan Bentley's neck squeezed between his hands. But Seamus beat him to it.

He didn't touch him. But then a man like Seamus didn't have to, to intimidate. He stepped right up into Alan's personal space, completely blocking Laurel and forcing Alan to step back.

"You cowardly little bastard."

"Dad, don't—"

He ignored her, continued putting himself quite impressively into Alan's personal space. Sean glanced down at his other scanner, just to assure himself that his readings were right and Alan wasn't carrying any weapon on his person, silently thanking the guys at Beauregard for letting him have access to such highly sensitive equipment. He'd thank them personally just as soon as he returned it before anyone noticed it had gone missing.

"I should have dealt with you directly the first time I got wind of your underhanded schemes. This will come as a surprise to you, I'm sure, but there have been people monitoring your actions for some time now."

Alan scoffed, but there wasn't much sincerity behind it. "Why should I believe that?"

"What you choose to believe is up to you, young man. But your days of blackmail and scamming are over."

"In my line of work, we trust evidence. You'll pardon me if I reserve judgment until I've seen a shred of it. Thus far, it's all been words."

"Sometimes, words are the most effective weapons. I've built my entire career on that belief." Seamus smiled, then shook his head and turned his back on Alan, as if he were no longer worth his time or attention.

He looked at Laurel, who was standing there somewhat speechless by the whole display. "Dad, how did you know about—"

He put his hand on her arm. "We'll talk about all that when this is done."

"You might as well have your little conversation now," Alan informed them, scraping together some semblance of superiority. "It might be your only chance."

Seamus didn't even bother glancing his way, which was the ultimate insult to someone like Bentley. His face began to turn red and his mouth tightened as if he were struggling to maintain his composure. "Do you not understand what I'm capable of? Who I am dealing with?"

Seamus said, "Excuse me" to Laurel, then turned to face Bentley once more. With his hands loosely linked in front of him, his legs braced wide, his demeanor so relaxed it bordered on jovial, Sean realized what an impressive prosecutor he must have made. And what a dangerous one he'd made, as well.

"I'm very aware of exactly who you are dealing with, although I'm not so certain you do. In fact, you might want to check in with them to see if they still feel your partnership with them is a viable one." He glanced at his watch. "Although they might be a bit busy at the moment."

"What in the hell are you talking about?"

"I'm talking about the raid presently under way on

a warehouse about twenty-five minutes from here. If all goes well, any number of the Rochambeau 'family' members are being taken into federal custody as we speak. In fact, a few hours from now, I imagine they'll be sufficiently caught up in trying to determine how to fight off the list of federal racketeering charges levied against them to not care overly much what trouble you may or may not be having with one recalcitrant judge.''

Alan swallowed hard then, and it was obvious he was scrabbling to gather every last scrap of bravado he had in him. "You must think I'm an idiot or something. You want me to think this is all over and give myself up." He laughed, but there was nothing remotely jovial or self-assured about the sound. "Well, there's something you should know about your daughter before you get too smug."

Laurel put her hand on her father's sleeve and began to move between them. Seamus held her back, but it didn't keep her from speaking. "All I ever wanted was for you to leave me alone. You refused. You dragged me into this because you were too weak to climb the ladder on your own strengths."

He snorted, then swung his gaze to Seamus. "I don't know if she told you, but she was here cutting a deal with me to get Jack Rochambeau off—again," he added with a sneer. "I guess it's something the Patricks make a habit of. I'm not the only one climbing into bed with the 'family.' In fact, it's getting mighty crowded in there."

Seamus reached for Bentley.

Laurel shrieked.

Sean came out of hiding.

14

"LET HIM GO, sir," Sean requested calmly, reaching inside his jacket.

"Who in the hell are you?" Bentley demanded, yanking himself from Seamus's grip.

Laurel spun around, both relieved and scared that Sean had abandoned his cover. She saw him reach inside his coat, move forward. "Sean, don't—"

Sean pulled out his badge, sending her a brief look. She'd thought he was going to pull a gun on them. He shook his head just slightly, chidingly, obviously aware of and amused by her assumption.

"State your business, young man," Seamus ordered.

Laurel's mouth dropped open. Her father hadn't known about this? About Sean? Then how in the hell—? She looked to Sean, who had obviously noted her surprise. That meant he now knew she'd thought he'd betrayed her. "I'm sorry," she mouthed silently.

He gave her a nod, a brief twitch of the lips, and she breathed a sigh of relief. It was going to be okay. What they had was stronger than a misunderstanding, a bad judgment call. She looked to her father then and realized fully just what Sean had been trying to tell her with that look. She and her father had that same bond. And it was strong enough to weather anything, even asking if one of them had made a mistake. No matter the severity or the potential fallout.

She felt even worse now for not fully comprehending that sooner, not trusting it. For not allowing her father to make his own decisions. For being too afraid to do what was right.

"Sean Gannon, Deputy U.S. Marshal."

"Are you here in some official capacity?" Seamus demanded.

Alan decided to use the sudden distraction to take a step back, then another one.

Sean swung his gaze toward him. "Stop right there."

Alan did just that, then made a face when he realized he'd responded so automatically. Laurel wasn't successful in hiding her satisfied little smile.

"Yes, sir," Sean answered Seamus, all the while keeping his gaze locked on Alan. "In a way. I'm here as your daughter's—" He stopped then, risked a glance over at her.

His face was so stern, so...Special Ops. Despite the intensity of the situation she'd been in, or perhaps because of it, she got a little sexual thrill out of it, out of seeing the other side of Sean in action. She stepped forward. "He's been helping me to sort out this mess." She put her hand on her dad's arm. "He wanted me to come to you sooner. I—I didn't want you to think... I wanted to just handle it myself and—"

Her father pulled her into his arms and held her tightly. "It's okay."

"It's not okay. I feel like I let you down. I *did* let you down. I let us both down. I'm so sorry, Dad."

He tipped up her chin and smiled down at her with

all the love and affection she'd always had from him gleaming from his blue eyes. "I think we both have a bit of owning up to do in that category." He glanced over at Sean. "Nice young man. He'll do."

He'd said it so casually, as if they weren't all standing there in some sort of frozen tableau of danger and suspense. It made her laugh. "Yes, that he will." She smiled. "It's all your fault, you know. I took your advice when I went to St. Thomas. Met an island man. And brought him home with me."

Alan stepped forward then, face almost purple. "You were with *him* in the islands? When you were still dealing with me? What kind of sl—"

Sean moved so fast Alan was standing one minute and flat on his face, hands pinned behind his back, the next. He was screaming bloody murder, threatening lawsuits with one breath and death threats with the next.

For his part, Sean appeared totally unmoved by the whole thing, keeping Alan contained almost nonchalantly.

The adrenaline that had been pumping through her system now for almost thirty straight minutes left Laurel feeling almost euphorically invincible. It was the only explanation for the way she all but swaggered over to where Alan lay pinned. She glanced at Sean. "I do so hope you still have that recorder running."

"Video and audio," he supplied with a calm that the bright gleam in his eye belied.

"Excellent." She nudged Alan with the toe of her high heel. "Yes, I was with him in the islands. In fact, I was with him in a way you only dreamed of being with me. There never was an 'us,' Alan. You don't know how to be part of a couple because that would mean that it's not all about you. And if anyone is going to throw around the slut word, I'm surprised it would be coming from you. A man who has consistently pimped himself out to the highest bidder."

Alan started a steady stream of invectives, which Sean neatly cut off with a little pressure to his windpipe. "Could you take the phone from my breast pocket and dial 9-1-1?" he asked Laurel, as if he were asking her to call for a pizza.

She slipped it out, took the time to drop a quick, hard kiss on his mouth, then did as he'd asked.

Response time was fast. In the several minutes it took the police to arrive, Seamus explained that his concern about Laurel had caused him to start poking around a bit. He'd called in every marker he'd earned over a long career, and that had been quite a few, and had eventually been made privy to the undercover investigation into Alan's wheelings and dealings. Concerned for his daughter's welfare, Seamus had called in some investigators of his own. He had no intention of impeding the investigation, so their job had been mostly to tail Alan and to make sure he was steering clear of Laurel. He only asked to be notified if Alan made any sort of direct contact. As it happened, he'd been on his way to Alexandria today, to be with her when news of the Rochambeau sting hit the wires, when Seamus's people had contacted him about the meeting going down at the bridge.

It took almost an hour of individual questioning before they were all cleared to leave the scene. Laurel had her left arm tucked inside her father's, and her head tilted to the right on Sean's shoulder. "I can't believe it's over," she said, shaky now that the adrenaline was diminishing.

Seamus paused as they walked back to their cars. "You know there will be more to come later. When this all comes to trial."

Laurel nodded. "Yes, but I can handle that."

Seamus beamed. "That's my girl."

Laurel tried to smile, but couldn't quite manage it. "Wait," she said, making them all come to a stop. "I know this isn't the time...well, actually it's way past time."

Her father had moved ahead of them a step, and turned back now to face the two of them. "What is it?" He hadn't missed the thread of anxiety in her tone. But then he didn't miss much.

"We have a lot to talk over, and this should probably wait until then, but it can't. I can't."

"Can't what, sweetheart?" Seamus asked, obviously concerned now.

Sean squeezed her hand and she turned to him. He smiled at her, his eyes alive with pride and love. He nodded, and she knew he realized what she was going to tell her father. "I love you," he said softly. "And so will he. Always."

Tears leaped to her eyes and she moved into Sean's arms, hugging him tightly. "I love you, too," she whispered fiercely next to his ear. "I'm sorry I doubted you."

"Shh," he said. "I told you once, I don't run."

She moved back, let her hands slide down his arms. "Neither do I. Not anymore." Then she took a breath and turned to face her father. With a tremble in her voice, she began. "I love you, Dad. More than you can know. More than that, I've always been proud of you, respected and admired you." She laughed a little, her voice catching. "I wanted to be you." Eyes swimming, she pushed on. "You did everything in your power to invest your love of the law into me. And it was such a powerful thing that I was entranced. But more important to me was making you proud."

Seamus's eyes had grown suspiciously bright. "But I am proud of you," he said, his voice rougher than usual. "I can't imagine being more proud."

Laurel felt her knees knocking, but she reached back and grabbed Sean's hand, tugged him forward until he was standing right beside her. "You asked Sean earlier who he was to me." She didn't look at Sean just then, couldn't chance it without risking falling completely apart. He tightened his hold on her hand, which was all the support she needed. "You have always been the man in my life, Dad. The one I looked up to. The center of my universe."

Seamus's mouth curved into a bit of a watery smile. "I take it I'm about to be told I've been replaced."

Laurel smiled through her own tears, happy tears. "Never. But you will have a little competition."

Sean stuck out his hand then. "I love your daughter, Your Honor. I'll never do anything to hurt her."

"Seamus," her father directed him, taking his hand in a firm shake. "And see that you don't."

Laurel sniffed, smiled, then continued. "Now for the hard part."

Seamus looked at her in surprise. "Do you love him?"

She did look at Sean now. "With all my heart."

"Then what more is there to know?"

"Just this. You said just now you were proud of me, couldn't imagine not being proud of me. Well..." She faltered, badly. She'd come so far, but it was so damn hard. Just a few words, but as her father had said, words were powerful things. And she hated the idea that hers were going to hurt him in any way.

"Go on," he urged. "You've come this far. Out with it."

She smiled at the autocratic tone, coupled with the love, affection and, yes, pride, so clear on his face. How could she have ever doubted it? "I know I've come a long way in my career," she began.

Seamus frowned, obviously a bit confused with the change of subject. It made it harder for her, but not impossible. She squeezed Sean's hand. No, she knew now that, with love, nothing was impossible.

"Would you have that same pride in me if I tell you that I've decided, after spending the first part of my life dedicated to following your career goals, I want to spend the next part of my life following Mom's?"

When Seamus only looked more confused, she spit it out more clearly.

"I want to step down, Dad, from the bench. I love the law, but I'm not in love with practicing it. I want to get married, build a home, a life, a partnership. And I don't want to divide my attentions." She glanced to Sean, whose returning look of unconditional love made her feel invincible all over again. Only this time it wasn't due to adrenaline. This was a feeling that wasn't going to fade away. As long as she had him by her side, she felt she could do anything. "I guess that wasn't the way I figured I'd propose, or be proposed to, but—"

Sean swept her up in his arms and planted one on her, right in front of her dad, God, and everybody. "I do," he said, then kissed her again. "I most certainly do."

Seamus finally cleared his throat and they both turned to him, faces flushed and eyes shining. "I never wanted to disappoint you, Dad. And I don't want to embarrass you by making a public thing of—"

"Hush now," he said gruffly, tugging her away from Sean and into a bear hug of his own. "Nothing you'll ever do will change how proud I am of you." He pushed her back a bit, stared down into her eyes. "You could have told me, you know," he quietly admonished. "More than anything, I've only wanted your happiness. I feel terrible knowing I forced you in any way to—"

"I made my own choices then, and I'm making my own choices now. I am happy, Dad. I don't think I've ever been happier."

"Then so am I." He smiled, that devilish gleam coming back into his eyes. "Of course, you think you had big shoes to fill in getting to the bench, you just try filling your mother's. You have a big challenge ahead of you there." He looked to Sean. "If I may, you might want to look into cooking lessons fairly soon."

Laurel swatted at her dad's arm. "Only if Sean goes with me. We're both hopeless in the kitchen."

Seamus, back to his outrageous self, shot a look at Sean. "So long as you're not hopeless in the—"

"Dad!"

They all laughed as they walked the rest of the way to their cars, Laurel holding hands with both of the men she held most dear.

Seamus left them at Sean's truck with a promise that they would be seeing each other soon to plan how they were going to stand up to the media explosion that was bound to take place over the next couple of days. "In the meantime," he called as he opened the door to his own sedan several yards away, "you might want to consider the idea of raising another generation of Patrick justices."

When they both just stared at him, nonplussed, his laughter boomed across the lot. He merely winked, waved and was still chuckling as he drove away.

"I can see now what you were up against," Sean muttered, sounding more awed than she'd ever heard him. "And I thought negotiating around my wolf pack of a family was a tough deal."

Laurel just shook her head. She should have known it wasn't going to be completely easy. But then nothing worth having ever was. She turned to Sean, moved into his arms. "Speaking of your den, when do I get to meet the Gannon pack?"

He pressed a kiss to her eyebrows, then her nose, her cheeks, her jaw… She'd almost forgotten the question by the time he got around to answering. "Oh, I was thinking you should be ready long about, hmm, when our youngest is in high school."

She laughed, her breath catching as she envisioned that future. A home filled with love, with children, with him. "What about at the wedding? Don't you think I should meet them before we—"

"Can't we just elope? Maybe to St. Thomas?"

She laughed. "What, and rob my father of walking me down the aisle? You're already robbing him of a justice."

He kissed her hard and fast. "Oh, I think we can work on giving him one or two more to terrorize." He kissed her again, only this time it turned gentle and heartbreakingly sweet. "A big wedding here," he said. "All the trimmings. And the terror of my family." He grinned. "Remember, you were warned." He leaned his back against the truck, pulling her between his legs. "Then a trip to St. Thomas. To finish what we started."

"Oh, I don't think this is ever going to be finished," she murmured, settling more fully against him before pulling his mouth down to hers.

And she was right.

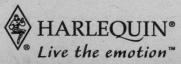

Is your man too good to be true?

Hot, gorgeous AND romantic?
If so, he could be a Harlequin® Blaze™ series cover model!

Our grand-prize winners will receive a trip for two to New York City to shoot the cover of a Blaze novel, and will stay at the luxurious Plaza Hotel. Plus, they'll receive $500 U.S. spending money! The runner-up winners will receive $200 U.S. to spend on a romantic dinner for two.

It's easy to enter!

In 100 words or less, tell us what makes your boyfriend or spouse a true romantic and the perfect candidate for the cover of a Blaze novel, and include in your submission two photos of this potential cover model.

All entries must include the written submission of the contest entrant, two photographs of the model candidate and the Official Entry Form and Publicity Release forms completed in full and signed by both the model candidate and the contest entrant. Harlequin, along with the experts at Elite Model Management, will select a winner.

For photo and complete Contest details, please refer to the Official Rules on the next page. All entries will become the property of Harlequin Enterprises Ltd. and are not returnable.

Please visit www.blazecovermodel.com to download a copy of the Official Entry Form and Publicity Release Form or send a request to one of the addresses below.

Please mail your entry to: **Harlequin Blaze Cover Model Search**

In U.S.A.	In Canada
P.O. Box 9069	P.O. Box 637
Buffalo, NY	Fort Erie, ON
14269-9069	L2A 5X3

No purchase necessary. Contest open to Canadian and U.S. residents who are 18 and over. Void where prohibited. Contest closes September 30, 2003.

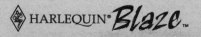

HARLEQUIN BLAZE COVER MODEL SEARCH CONTEST 3569 OFFICIAL RULES
NO PURCHASE NECESSARY TO ENTER

1. To enter, submit two (2) 4" x 6" photographs of a boyfriend or spouse (who must be 18 years of age or older) taken no later than three (3) months from the time of entry: a close-up, waist up, shirtless photograph; and a fully clothed, full-length photograph, then, tell us, in 100 words or fewer, why he should be a Harlequin Blaze cover model and how he is romantic. Your complete "entry" must include: (i) your essay, (ii) the Official Entry Form and Publicity Release Form printed below completed and signed by you (as "Entrant"), (iii) the photographs (with your hand-written name, address and phone number, and your model's name, address and phone number on the back of each photograph), and (iv) the Publicity Release Form and Photograph Representation Form printed below completed and signed by your model (as "Model"), and should be sent via first-class mail to either: Harlequin Blaze Cover Model Search Contest 3569, P.O. Box 9069, Buffalo, NY, 14269-9069, or Harlequin Blaze Cover Model Search Contest 3569, P.O. Box 637, Fort Erie, Ontario L2A 5X3. All submissions must be in English and be received no later than September 30, 2003. Limit: one entry per person, household or organization. **Purchase or acceptance of a product offer does not improve your chances of winning.** All entry requirements must be strictly adhered to for eligibility and to ensure fairness among entries.

2. Ten (10) Finalist submissions (photographs and essays) will be selected by a panel of judges consisting of members of the Harlequin editorial, marketing and public relations staff, as well as a representative from Elite Model Management (Toronto) Inc., based on the following criteria:

Aptness/Appropriateness of submitted photographs for a Harlequin Blaze cover—70%
Originality of Essay—20%
Sincerity of Essay—10%

In the event of a tie, duplicate finalists will be selected. The photographs submitted by finalists will be posted on the Harlequin website no later than November 15, 2003 (at www.blazecovermodel.com), and viewers may vote, in rank order, on their favorite(s) to assist in the panel of judges' final determination of the Grand Prize and Runner-up winning entries based on the above judging criteria. All decisions of the judges are final.

3. All entries become the property of Harlequin Enterprises Ltd. and none will be returned. Any entry may be used for future promotional purposes. Elite Model Management (Toronto) Inc. and/or its partners, subsidiaries and affiliates operating as "Elite Model Management" will have access to all entries including all personal information, and may contact any Entrant and/or Model in its sole discretion for their own business purposes. Harlequin and Elite Model Management (Toronto) Inc. are separate entities with no legal association or partnership whatsoever having no power to bind or obligate the other or create any expressed or implied obligation or responsibility on behalf of the other, such that Harlequin shall not be responsible in any way for any acts or omissions of Elite Model Management (Toronto) Inc. or its partners, subsidiaries and affiliates in connection with the Contest or otherwise and Elite Model Management shall not be responsible in any way for any acts or omissions of Harlequin or its partners, subsidiaries and affiliates in connection with the contest or otherwise.

4. All Entrants and Models must be residents of the U.S. or Canada, be 18 years of age or older, and have no prior criminal convictions. The contest is not open to any Model that is a professional model and/or actor in any capacity at the time of the entry. Contest void wherever prohibited by law; all applicable laws and regulations apply. Any litigation within the Province of Quebec regarding the conduct or organization of a publicity contest may be submitted to the Régie des alcools, des courses et des jeux for a ruling, and any litigation regarding the awarding of a prize may be submitted to the Régie only for the purpose of helping the parties reach a settlement. Employees and immediate family members of Harlequin Enterprises Ltd., D.L. Blair, Inc., Elite Model Management (Toronto) Inc. and their parents, affiliates, subsidiaries and all other agencies, entities and persons connected with the use, marketing or conduct of this Contest are not eligible to enter. Acceptance of any prize offered constitutes permission to use Entrants' and Models' names, essay submissions, photographs or other likenesses for the purposes of advertising, trade, publication and promotion on behalf of Harlequin Enterprises Ltd., its parent, affiliates, subsidiaries, assigns and other authorized entities involved in the judging and promotion of the contest without further compensation to any Entrant or Model, unless prohibited by law.

5. Finalists will be determined no later than October 30, 2003. Prize Winners will be determined no later than January 31, 2004. Grand Prize Winners (consisting of winning Entrant and Model) will be required to sign and return Affidavit of Eligibility/Release of Liability and Model Release forms within thirty (30) days of notification. Non-compliance with this requirement and within the specified time period will result in disqualification and an alternate will be selected. Any prize notification returned as undeliverable will result in the awarding of the prize to an alternate set of winners. All travelers (or parent/legal guardian of a minor) must execute the Affidavit of Eligibility/Release of Liability prior to ticketing and must possess required travel documents (e.g. valid photo ID) where applicable. Travel dates specified by Sponsor but no later than May 30, 2004.

6. Prizes: One (1) Grand Prize—the opportunity for the Model to appear on the cover of a paperback book from the Harlequin Blaze series, and a 3 day/2 night trip for two (Entrant and Model) to New York, NY for the photo shoot of Model which includes round-trip coach air transportation from the commercial airport nearest the winning Entrant's home to New York, NY, (or, in lieu of air transportation, $100 cash payable to Entrant and Model, if the winning Entrant's home is within 250 miles of New York, NY), hotel accommodations (double occupancy) at the Plaza Hotel and $500 cash spending money payable to Entrant and Model, (approximate prize value: $8,000), and one (1) Runner-up Prize of $200 cash payable to Entrant and Model for a romantic dinner for two (approximate prize value: $200). Prizes are valued in U.S. currency. Prizes consist of only those items listed as part of the prize. No substitution of prize(s) permitted by winners. All prizes are awarded jointly to the Entrant and Model of the winning entries, and are not severable - prizes and obligations may not be assigned or transferred. Any change to the Entrant and/or Model of the winning entries will result in disqualification and an alternate will be selected. Taxes on prize are the sole responsibility of winners. Any and all expenses and/or items not specifically described as part of the prize are the sole responsibility of winners. Harlequin Enterprises Ltd. and D.L. Blair, Inc., their parents, affiliates, and subsidiaries are not responsible for errors in printing of Contest entries and/or game pieces. No responsibility is assumed for lost, stolen, late, illegible, incomplete, inaccurate, non-delivered, postage due or misdirected mail or entries. In the event of printing or other errors which may result in unintended prize values or duplication of prizes, all affected game pieces or entries shall be null and void.

7. Winners will be notified by mail. For winners' list (available after March 31, 2004), send a self-addressed, stamped envelope to: Harlequin Blaze Cover Model Search Contest 3569 Winners, P.O. Box 4200, Blair, NE 68009-4200, or refer to the Harlequin website (at www.blazecovermodel.com).

Contest sponsored by Harlequin Enterprises Ltd., P.O. Box 9042, Buffalo, NY 14269-9042.

HBCVRMODEL2

eHARLEQUIN.com

The eHarlequin.com online community is *the* place to share opinions, thoughts and feelings!

- Joining the community is easy, fun and **FREE!**

- Connect with **other romance fans** on our message boards.

- Meet your **favorite authors** without leaving home!

- **Share opinions** on books, movies, celebrities...and *more!*

Here's what our members say:

"I love the friendly and helpful atmosphere filled with support and humor."
—Texanna (eHarlequin.com member)

"Is this the place for me, or what? There is nothing I love more than 'talking' books, especially with fellow readers who are reading the same ones I am."
—Jo Ann (eHarlequin.com member)

Join today by visiting www.eHarlequin.com!

If you enjoyed what you just read,
then we've got an offer you can't resist!

Take 2 bestselling love stories FREE!

Plus get a FREE surprise gift!

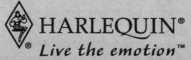

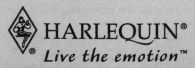